His organs were melting inside him. He was aware of nothing but his chest, filling with bubbling bile that moved and swished like rioting waves. He coughed and gagged, retched and hacked. He sank back down to the ground. He wanted to scream – in confusion, in terror and, most of all, in agony – but he was unable.

His lungs were gone. He was completely hollow inside. But he was not dead.

Not quite.

With special thanks to James Noble

ORCHARD BOOKS

338 Euston Road, London NW1 3BH
Orchard Books Australia
Level 17/207 Kent St, Sydney, NSW 2000
A Paperback Original

First published in Great Britain in 2011

A CIP catalogue record for this book is available from
the British Library.

ISBN 978 1 40831 3 886
1 3 5 7 9 10 8 6 4 2

Printed in Great Britain by CPI Bookmarque, Croydon

The paper and board used in this paperback are natural recyclable
products made from wood grown in sustainable forests. The
manufacturing processes conform to the environmental regulations
of the country of origin.

Orchard Books is a division of Hachette Children's Books,
an Hachette UK company
www.hachette.co.uk

ROBIN HOOD vs THE PLAGUE UNDEAD

James Black

ORCHARD BOOKS

Prologue

Nottingham, England. October 1194 AD

George ran. There was nothing else left to do.

He ran so fast, his breath lodged itself like a dagger in his chest. His lungs ached. His skull throbbed and pounded with tiredness and panic. It was a cold night in early October, but hot sweat ran down his face, neck and back.

He had not wanted to break curfew – the town law that forbid anyone from leaving their houses after nightfall – but his friend Harry had said that the sergeants did not patrol their street at night. Harry had said they could go exploring, looking for buried treasure – he was always yapping on about the old Saxons burying treasure when William the Conqueror took control of England, so the nasty Normans couldn't get their hands on it.

Harry said it would be fun. He said there was nothing to worry about.

Harry was wrong.

And now he was dead.

When he couldn't run any more, George slowed to

a stop and looked around. He squinted, trying to see through the darkness, but it was impossible. The autumn sky had been thick with clouds during the day, and now the moon and stars hid behind them.

He knew he was on a residential street, but he had no idea which one – or what way he would have to run to get home.

'Help!' George called, his voice weak.

But no one came.

Everything was quiet, as it always was after curfew. In a city like Nottingham, the people lived only to work, and they worked hard. Ten, twelve hours a day. When they got home, they slept soundly. And even if his call woke someone up, George knew that they would be too frightened of being caught outside after dark to answer it.

'Help...' he gasped.

Someone answered. But it was not anyone George was hoping for.

He turned at the sound of ragged, rhythm-less footsteps. They were coming from behind him.

George knew it was not help coming his way, but death. Cruel, painful death – the same that had fallen on poor Harry. He could not see it – not all of it. Its body was hidden behind the curtain of darkness, but its eyes peered through. Mismatched eyes, one a dull grey, the other crying thin tears of blood. Their faint, hideous glow lit up the thing's face, showing half-rotted skin peeling away in flaps, showing bits of the skull beneath.

It looked like someone who had died of a plague. Someone who had died without their body realising it.

'Please, leave me alone. I'm just a boy!'

George ran. There was nothing else left to do.

He ran, knowing he could not run much longer.

The thing ran after him.

It was getting closer.

Part One

Chapter One

Robin Hood moved through Sherwood Forest as silently as a spirit. His bow was slung over one broad shoulder, and his legs carried him forward in great strides. He swept his long brown hair out of his eyes, as he tracked a trundling steel-wheeled cart loaded with a dozen canvas sacks. At the head of the cart sat a squat, chinless man with sandy hair and a pot belly that bulged through his tunic. He was guiding a chestnut horse along the Nottingham Road as it curved away to the West.

Robin joined his friend, Little John, who was crouched behind a birch tree with his double-headed axe held in his meaty fist.

'What do you think?' Robin whispered.

'Looks like grain,' said Little John, who was not 'little' at all, but the tallest man Robin had ever met. He was huge – his arms were long enough to wrap around a tree trunk, and strong enough that he could probably uproot it and toss it twenty yards.

Little John squinted as he looked at the cart

rumbling past. 'I've never seen this man before.'

Robin clapped his friend on the back. 'Then let's ask him some questions.'

They set off at a run, picking up the pace and trusting that the clattering cartwheels would mask the sound of their approach.

Robin, the faster of the two, slipped behind the cart as its wheels sprayed up clumps of earth and shards of broken wood. With the horse at a walk, he had no trouble catching up, and jumped gracefully into the cart.

The chinless man felt the cart lurch. In the time it took him to cast a fearful look over his shoulder, Robin had already slipped his bow into his hands and strung an arrow.

'Stop the cart,' said Robin, 'or you'll get the King Harold treatment.'

The man did not need telling twice. He yanked hard on the reins, bringing his horse to a stop.

As Little John caught up with them, Robin hopped off the cart, keeping his arrow unerringly trained on the chinless man's eye.

'What's your name?' Robin asked him.

'G-G-Godfrey, sir,' said the man, looking from Robin to Little John. He gasped at the sight of the seven-foot Outlaw, who looked like a mountain with a beard.

Robin nodded at Little John, who lowered his axe down to waist height.

'And what brings you along this road?' Robin asked.

'I'm bound for Nottingham,' said Godfrey. 'Going to sell my grain – see?' He turned and pointed at the sacks.

Robin and Little John looked them over. 'Twelve sacks,' Robin commented. 'You've room for lots more.'

Godfrey nodded. 'Yes. I did have more, but I've already sold much of it in Lincoln.'

'Oh, aye?' said Little John. 'So Nottingham gets the stale stuff, does it?'

'No!' Godfrey squeaked, shaking his head so violently he almost fell off his cart. 'You misunderstand—'

'He's just joking with you, Godfrey,' said Robin, reaching into the cart and patting the nearest sack. Godfrey gripped the reins of his carthorse so tight that Robin thought he'd soon draw blood from his palms.

'You wouldn't rob me, would you?' Godfrey asked.

'That depends,' said Robin, stepping back from the cart.

'On what?' said Godfrey.

'What happens when my friend rips one of these sacks open.'

Little John swung his axe at the nearest sack, splitting the canvas and sending grain spilling out onto the cart.

Grain – and silver coins.

'Well, well!' said Little John. 'This is unlike any grain I've ever seen before. Must be fancy French stuff, eh?'

Robin looked at Godfrey and saw his eyes darting in each direction. 'I... I...' he stammered. 'I search for the one they call Robin Hood. I bring him a great gift.'

'Well, you've found him,' said Robin.

Godfrey tried to jump off the cart, but his foot tangled itself up in the reins and he was flipped in midair. He hit the ground hard. Robin thought he heard a rib crack. But that did not stop Godfrey, who struggled up to his knees. 'Good Robin of Sherwood,' he said, 'I bring you the gift of money that I stole from a tax collector along this very road. Almost a thousand silver coins to swell your noble Outlaws' treasury.'

Robin and Little John shared a glance over the

man's head. With just their eyes, they asked each other: does this man look capable of robbing a tax collector by himself?

Robin slung his bow back over his shoulder and looked down at Godfrey. 'An impressive feat,' he said. 'You should be proud of your courage.'

'I follow your example, good Robin,' said Godfrey. 'You are an inspiration.'

Robin cast another glance at Little John, seeing the big man share his smirk. 'Oh, yes, I know,' he said. 'An inspiration. That's me, alright.' He extended his hand. 'On your feet, brother Godfrey.'

Godfrey raised his head, gratitude and relief swelling his face so fervently he almost seemed to grow a chin. He clasped the proffered hand firmly. 'Thank you, Robin!'

As he helped the man to his feet, Robin curled his hand over Godfrey's forearm with snake-like speed. He stabbed his fingers into his sleeve, finding what he was looking for – parchment, tied around Godfrey's wrist with twine. Robin had it free in an instant. He stepped away from Godfrey. Little John crept up behind Godfrey and lowered his axe shaft over his head, holding him tight by the chest.

'Robin, sir!' cried Godfrey. 'Don't misunderstand—'

'Oh, there's little chance of that,' said Robin, as he unfolded the parchment, revealing a list of names. English names. Most had been crossed out; the ones that had not were marked with tiny crosses.

Robin had encountered many tax collectors, and he knew what their lists looked like. The crosses indicated the people who could not pay – the people who would soon be arrested and thrown into the Sheriff of Nottingham's dungeon. If not worse.

'Oh, yes, I understand perfectly,' said Robin. 'A clever ruse, Godfrey. You think fast on your feet – but I think faster. You were taking this money to the Sheriff of Nottingham.' He held the parchment up. 'You are the tax collector.'

'Norman scum!' barked Little John, moving the axe shaft up to Godfrey's throat.

'No!' Godfrey gasped, as Little John lifted him right off his feet.

'Save your breath!' said John. 'You'll need it to tell the Sheriff a more believable lie than the one you just told us.'

'Oh, he won't need to lie, John,' said Robin, stepping up to the cart. 'I'm sure our fine Sheriff will have no trouble believing that this is the work of the Sherwood Outlaws.'

'Aye, right enough, Robin,' said John, putting more pressure on Godfrey's throat. The tax collector was starting to turn purple.

'Let him go, John,' said Robin, reaching into the cart and dragging towards him two of the canvas bags. He removed two drawstrings, seeing more grain and silver coins spill out on to the wood with a clatter that echoed in the forest. As Little John held Godfrey in place, Robin knelt to tie one of the strings tightly around the tax collector's ankles. Then he tied the man's hands behind his back.

Little John released Godfrey with a shove. The bulbous Norman was helpless to stop himself falling flat on his face with a dull thud. He wriggled and writhed as he tried to right himself. Robin and Little John laughed so much they had to lean against the cart.

'Is that a Norman style of walking, Robin?' said Little John, with a wicked grin. 'It must take them ages to get anywhere!'

Robin took two handfuls of Godfrey's tunic and sat him upright. 'Now, then,' he said. 'I'm going to set you on your feet, so you can hop all the way to the Sheriff's castle. But before I do, I want to make sure you know exactly why we have done this to you.'

Godfrey's face had completely lost all pretence of pleading, his expression replaced with indignant hatred. 'Because you're a Saxon turd,' he snarled. 'King of the peasants.'

Robin tutted. He had heard a lot worse. 'Please don't take my actions personally,' he said. 'I'm sure that, when you're not out taking Englishmen's hard-earned money, you're a decent man. But you work for the Sheriff and his puppet master, Prince John. That makes you my enemy. Tell the Sheriff that Robin Hood said if he so desperately wants a thousand silver coins, he should ask his rich Norman friends to spare him a few, rather than beat it out of the English poor.'

Robin helped Godfrey to his feet. The tax collector swayed for a moment, but Robin steadied him and turned him West, in the direction of the Sheriff's castle.

'On your way, Godfrey,' said Robin, as he took a handful of the horse's reins and began leading the cart in the other direction. 'And be careful as you hop along the road. Next time you fall, there will be no friendly Saxons to help you up.'

Laughing heartily, Robin joined Little John, who was leading their new horse and cart into the depths of the forest. His big friend clapped him on the back, sending Robin stumbling forward a few steps.

'A thousand coins, eh?' said Little John. 'We could retire on that.'

'But we won't,' said Robin. 'The money will go back to the people the Sheriff has taken it from. Won't it?'

Little John sighed as he kept walking. 'Aye... I suppose.'

Chapter Two

'A thousand coins!'

The Sheriff of Nottingham paced the Great Hall of his castle, his boots trampling the straw covering the stone slabs, sending up puffs of dust and dirt.

Godfrey the tax collector was kneeling in front of him with his head bowed.

The Sheriff knew his gaze was hard for most men to hold. He had been blessed with coal-black eyes that contrasted sharply with his pale, almost cherub-like Norman features. 'Satan's eyes set deep into an Angel's face.' That was how he was most often described by the people of Nottingham. Behind his back, of course.

'*Look at me!*' snarled the Sheriff.

Godfrey finally found the Sheriff's gaze. He even managed to hold it for a few seconds – the Sheriff was almost impressed.

'You let Robin Hood humiliate me, you chinless cretin,' the Sheriff said. 'Now, my name will be a joke throughout Nottingham – and probably beyond!' His swinging foot caught the underside of Godfrey's jaw, lifting him off the ground. Godfrey crashed through a trestle table; the sound of his teeth raining on the wood debris was loud in the empty Great Hall.

The Great Hall used to be the heart of the Sheriff's castle, bustling with servants, knights and sergeants – but not any more. Now, the Sheriff needed the Great Hall to be a place of secrecy. No one was allowed in without his permission.

'Oh, do go easy on him.'

The Sheriff froze, eyes still on the now toothless tax collector, but barely seeing him. He planted his hand cautiously on the hilt of his sword as he turned in the direction of the shrill voice.

Mother Maudlin, the Witch of Paplewick, stood on the Great Hall's high table, though the Sheriff had not heard her enter. Her black robe was so long it hung over the edge of the table; her hair flowed down to her waist, and was so blonde it was almost white. She looked no older than twenty, but the Sheriff had heard whispers that she was at least four times that age.

Everything about her face was unnatural, like a mask of a woman sculpted by someone with an unsteady hand. Her porcelain-pale skin was wrapped as tight as a drum around sharp cheekbones and a jaw that was almost perfectly triangular, her chin as pointed as the tip of a spear. Her sky-blue eyes were like none the Sheriff had ever seen before, and they blazed in the gloom of the Great Hall at dusk. In the centre of her forehead was carved a five-pointed star. The pus that leaked from it caught the torchlight.

'I've told you before,' said the Sheriff, 'stop sneaking up on me like that.'

'And I've told you before,' said the Witch, 'you no longer have the authority to execute useful men.'

'Useful men?' the Sheriff sneered. 'He's a failure. A disgrace.'

Mother Maudlin moved in half the time it took the Sheriff to blink. One moment she was on the table, the next she was standing in front of him, with a wry smile twisting her lips. The Sheriff recoiled at the stench of the pus draining from the pentagram scar.

'Don't you remember your promise to Prince John?' she asked, her voice dragged down to a raspy whisper. A teasing, taunting glint filled her unnatural eyes. 'You guaranteed a thousand able-bodied men for his army. A thousand souls.'

'Of course I remember,' snapped the Sheriff. 'But I don't think he'll miss one imbecilic tax collector.'

'That is not for you to decide,' said Mother Maudlin, shaking her head.

'I must be allowed to keep order in Nottingham,' the Sheriff insisted. 'I still give the orders here.'

'For now,' said the Witch. 'But Prince John's plan is bigger than Nottingham, my good Sheriff. He plays for the future of England – which means that it is for the Prince to decide who joins his…army.'

At this, Godfrey struggled forward and threw himself down in front of Mother Maudlin. 'My lady, I will gladly serve the Prince.'

Maudlin stole a glance at the Sheriff, her eyes alight with cruel humour. 'You know what to do,' she said.

The Sheriff grabbed the protesting Godfrey by his neck and dragged him down torch-lit corridors into the castle dungeon.

'My lord Sheriff,' Godfrey whimpered as he bumped down the spiral staircase. 'Please! Have mercy! I volunteer to serve the Prince!'

The staircase led to a wide, cavernous chamber beneath the castle. In the centre of the floor yawned a hole fifteen foot deep, covered with an iron grill. This was the Sheriff's specially constructed dungeon – he enjoyed the sound of his prisoners begging for mercy. Their echoing calls of distress helped him sleep.

'You *will* serve the Prince, Godfrey,' said Mother

Maudlin, who had appeared in the dungeon ahead of them, even though the Sheriff had left her behind in the Great Hall not two minutes ago. 'You will serve him very well.'

The Sheriff grappled with the tax collector as he fought to free himself. 'Please!' he wailed, as the Sheriff bundled him towards the far left cell. 'Have mercy!'

'Shut up!' snarled the Sheriff, turning the portly man round as he drew his sword. He slammed the hilt into the tax collector's temple and let him fall to the floor, unconscious.

The Sheriff looked into the dungeon. Mother Maudlin stood on the edge of the hole, gazing through the rusty bars. The Sheriff joined her, willing his eyes not to clamp shut at the sight of the *thing* inside the cell.

A man crouched in the corner on all fours, like a wild dog. He wore the chain-mail of a sergeant, and a cloak with the Sheriff's colours – black and red – but it was covered in blood, mucus, bile and anything else a body expelled at the point of death. He turned his face up to the Sheriff. One of his eyes wept blood, while the other was just a dead, greyish orb. Fissures ripped through the skin of his face, his neck, his forearms, revealing rotting flesh and muscle, even slithers of bone. His hands were gnarled, claw-like, scratching at the earthen floor as he grunted and growled.

The Sheriff looked to the other side of the dungeon and saw a sight that made him retch. He didn't know why he bothered to hold his breakfast down – it was not like he could make the stench any worse.

'He mauled the boy,' the Sheriff said, pointing at the servant he had thrown into the cell earlier that morning. The boy lay face down in a pool of his own blood, the flesh of his legs picked clean off the bones. 'You said you had that *thing* under control,' the Sheriff said, indicating the sergeant.

'I *do* have it under control,' replied the Witch.

'Well, it doesn't look like it,' said the Sheriff.

Mother Maudlin fixed the Sheriff with a grin that made him step back. 'Many things aren't apparent to you, Sheriff. You're just a tool, a weapon, in this great plan.'

'If I had known from the start,' said the Sheriff, still looking into the pit, 'that the Prince was working with *you*, well...'

Mother Maudlin giggled. 'Don't deceive yourself. You would have still thrown yourself at the Prince's feet and begged to be involved,' she said. 'And you know it – the power the Prince has promised you once he becomes King is just too irresistible to a greedy soul such as yours.'

The Sheriff did not argue. The Witch was right, and he hated her for it.

He pointed into the dungeon. 'It does not change what has happened here,' he said. 'You promised your...creature...wouldn't kill the boy.'

'He didn't.'

The Witch's eyes rolled back inside her skull, revealing the whites, which glowed like the moon. She spread her arms, the palms of her hands turning up towards the ceiling, fingers curling into claws. Her sleeves rode up her arms, revealing a map of weeping sores that puckered and pulsed in her skin, leaking the same rancid pus that trickled from the pentagram in her forehead.

The stench awoke awful memories in the Sheriff's mind – memories he had tried in vain to forget. He remembered the Witch pouring her pus into a goblet and forcing it down the sergeant's throat; the sergeant who now lived like a wild animal in his dungeon.

The wet, hissing noise now emanating from the Witch's mouth, he instinctively knew to be a call to the creature. Mother Maudlin slowly lowered her head.

When the Sheriff followed her gaze, however, he saw not the sergeant but the dead boy's shoulders twitch and shudder, his head rising off the dirty floor, to reveal a face bearing the same affliction as the sergeant who had killed him – one dead grey eye, the other leaking blood; the boils; the pallid complexion. His clawed hands reached for the rough walls of the dungeon as he dragged his flayed body along the ground, pulling himself to his bony feet.

The boy had no flesh on his legs, his lower torso hanging over his hips like a torn curtain, and yet he stood up in defiance of the death that he should have suffered.

The Sheriff made to cross himself, and then thought better of it. God would not forgive him now. Not for *this*.

'Another Undead to add to the ranks,' said Mother Maudlin wistfully. 'And I will control them. But they need to feed – to keep their strength up. Otherwise my poor babies will get all sluggish and listless.'

As the Sheriff swallowed down more bile, Mother Maudlin looked at him. 'I sense hesitance,' she said. 'You are reconsidering.'

'I'm trying to understand how this will work,' the Sheriff said. 'How can we infect the citizens of

Nottingham *efficiently*? You say the bite of the Undead will give people your plague?'

'Yes,' hissed Mother Maudlin.

'But there's a thousand people or more in Nottingham,' said the Sheriff, unable to keep the condescension out of his own voice. 'And these Saxon peasants will flee the city at the first sight of any plague. Your plan has many flaws, Mother.'

Mother Maudlin's eyes never left the Sheriff's. 'That is not my problem. I don't care how you do it, Sheriff,' she said. 'Just as long as it is done. One thousand souls.' And before he could answer, she smiled even wider, her eyes unearthly lighting up the dungeon with a hideous glow. 'And be swift about it! The Prince himself will be here in eight days.'

'Prince John makes for Nottingham?' the Sheriff blurted out, instantly cursing himself. He was acting like hired help, not an equal conspirator – which he was. Of course he was. After all, look at all the work he was doing.

'Yes, he does,' said Mother Maudlin with a casual flap of her hand. 'So you had better make good on your promise within that time. Hadn't you?'

The Sheriff could have happily thrown the Witch into the dungeon. The arrogance in her voice enraged him. His fingers twitched over his sword hilt.

But can I slay her with my sword? he asked himself. *Could I kill her? She is getting too powerful for my liking.*

He knew he would have to tread very carefully from now on.

Godfrey the tax collector did not feel himself being thrown into the dungeon with the Undead. Nor did he feel their clawed hands scratching at his face, or their hideous, blood-stained teeth sink into his neck and belly.

He did not feel them move away from him at Mother Maudlin's command, and he did not feel the swift pox rampage through his veins like an invading army. The Plague was in his blood, driving him to the edge of life and dangling him over the abyss that was death.

But he was not dropped over the edge. He was left dangling.

The first thing he felt was the burning; a searing sensation in the bite marks on his neck and belly. The fire in Godfrey's flesh radiated outwards from the wounds. He could feel his hot, sticky blood flowing from his body.

His knees and thighs protested with silent, interior screams of agony as he tried to push himself to his feet; the back of his head pounded incessantly, and his neck refused to move more than a few degrees in either direction.

Standing upright, Godfrey rubbed his face to clear away the streaming sweat and felt the boils on his forehead. He ran his fingertips over them, finding that they formed arches over his eyes before snaking down his cheeks, oozing pus that mixed with the sweat and ran off his chin.

He was still burning. All over. Inside and out. He panted like a dog as he tried to suck air into his lungs, his hands tearing his tunic. But it did no good. The fire inside would not be doused, and could not be snuffed out.

His legs couldn't bear his weight for more than a few seconds. They collapsed like rotten wood and he hit the damp earth of the pit, simultaneously overcome with a delirious confusion and a petulant acceptance.

He was dying. He could feel it. It was an immense sensation, terrifying and all-consuming.

His heart beat rapidly, without rhythm. Boiling blood roared in his ears as his pulse pounded in his chest, his wrist, his neck, his head.

He sat bolt upright as fierce pain sliced through him, like a dozen daggers dug deep in his gut.

It was his organs. They were melting. Melting inside him. He pitched forward in his sitting position, suddenly aware of nothing but his chest, filling with a bubbling bile that moved and swished like rioting waves. He coughed and gagged, retched and hacked; his chest heaved once, twice. On the third, his useless, melted human organs ejected themselves in a stream of oozing black sludge that scalded his flesh on the inside. Up and up they came, streaked with lashings of blood and phlegm, the mess slowly rolling away, forming a viscous mound that frothed and plopped like boiling water in a pot.

The vomiting continued, endlessly, the final dregs of Godfrey's internal human body weakly dribbling out of him. He spluttered and tried to get up again, finding himself powerless to do so. His flesh and bones were dead weight, and his muscles refused to work. He sank back down to the ground. He wanted to scream – in confusion, in terror and, most of all, in agony – but he was unable.

His lungs were gone. He was completely hollow inside. But he was not dead.

Not quite.

Chapter Three

One week later

It was the middle of the afternoon when Robin Hood returned to Sherwood Forest from a clandestine visit to the fair at Nottingham. He walked as cautiously as ever, making sure he was not tracked to his band's secret camp by double-backing on himself, and keeping a sharp ear out for anyone who might be following him.

Not that there was much chance of that happening once Robin moved off the beaten, muddy paths that sliced through the vast woodland – not once he set foot among the dense birch trees. To the untrained eye, the trees were an incomprehensible labyrinth; their tops merging together to roof the forest from the sun, making it near-impossible to tell the time of the day. Two paces off the path, a stranger would be lost.

But the forest held no surprises for Robin Hood. He had walked among the trees for the best part of seven years, since the day he was outlawed and exiled here; to him, each tree was unique, a signpost guiding him back to his secret camp.

He knew every tree, every dip and swell of the ground beneath his feet. He could tell the time of day from the angle of the sunlight as it slipped through the canopy. He could tell the season from the smell of the air. He knew every sound – from the sing-song call of the birds, to the thudding of a deer's hooves punching the earth. Great Sherwood was a secluded country unto itself, and Robin was the closest thing it had to a king.

So when he saw or heard something in the depths of Sherwood that should not have been there, he paid attention. What he heard was the sound of heavy breathing – human. Robin flattened himself against the nearest birch tree, slipping the longbow off his shoulder and reaching for an arrow from his quiver.

He peered around the sturdy trunk, seeking the source of the sound. He found it, right where he knew it would be – about thirty paces northwest. Crouched at the foot of a tree with his bow angled towards the earth and shoulders tense with fear, was Much the Miller's Son – the youngest of Robin's Outlaws.

So, Much had been elected to go hunting today, Robin thought.

The young Outlaw was not the best of hunters, and it showed – he constantly shifted his position as he sought comfort, his rump digging a crater in the earth, his feet snapping and crushing dropped twigs and dried leaves.

He was making a lot of noise – any deer nearby had surely fled a long time ago.

Robin grinned to himself, pondering a way to scare the wits out of the lad. An arrow an inch from his floppy brown fringe, perhaps?

Robin's back stiffened when he heard the sound of three men walking stealthily. Robin knew that the only men able to move through its depths with any confidence were his Outlaws. But if these had been his Outlaws, one of them would have called out to signal their presence.

Robin had heard no call – which meant, these footsteps belonged to strangers.

And the only strangers who would have reason to come this deep into Sherwood were the foresters. Fear flooded Robin's chest – all deer belonged to England's ruler, King Richard, and to hunt in the woodlands was a capital offence. The foresters were commissioned by the Crown, and they had the right to kill poachers.

Robin looked at Much. The youngster had also heard the approaching foresters and he was shifting anxiously, considering whether to flee or hide.

Robin darted from tree to tree, getting closer to his friend, hoping that the boy's gaze would turn to him. But Much's eyes seemed to go everywhere but towards him.

When he was only three trees away, Robin saw Much's eyes widen and dart this way and that. Much was having an idea.

That was never a good thing.

Before Robin could hiss a warning to him, Much leaned as far around his tree as he could without being seen. He took a deep breath and whooped. '*Ahwooo!*' He was hoping to scare the foresters away by howling like a wolf.

It was all Robin could do not to bang his head against the tree. Much's impression was more like a frightened puppy. The Foresters' footsteps ceased for a second, then they resumed – quicker, and getting louder, running right towards the young Outlaw.

'Poacher!' cried one of them, as Robin heard the drawing of swords.

'Catch him!' yelled another.

Poor, hapless Much scrambled to his feet, which almost got tangled in his long cloak. Robin shook his head as he saw the lad's course: west, towards the Outlaws' camp.

'There he is!' shouted the first voice. Robin peered round his tree and saw who it belonged to. The stoutest of the foresters, in the middle of the three-man line. He was bulky, barely able to fit into his woollen tunic and flowing black cloak, his log-sized legs pumping furiously as he and his two smaller companions pursued Much.

Robin continued darting from tree to tree, tracking the chase and waiting for his moment to pounce. The foresters were gaining on Much.

Robin could have shot them. Even moving targets were easy for him, but Robin was no murderer, no matter what the Sheriff of Nottingham tried to tell the people.

Much at last seemed to realise that holding his bow in one hand might be slowing him down, and so brought it up over his shoulder. But the string snagged on the back of Much's neck, and Robin saw the bow fly once all the way round his head.

The young Outlaw stumbled to a stop, turning towards Foresters, his face reddening. The bowstring had wrapped tight around his neck.

The Foresters caught up with him in seconds. When they stopped running, the silence was so heavy, Robin had to come to a complete stop and hold his breath to make sure he was not heard.

'Look at this, lads,' said the biggest one, as Much sank to his knees, his face reddening as his slender fingers tried to loosen the bowstring. 'He's executing himself!'

The foresters chortled as Much pitched forward. Stray spittle spewed from his lips. Robin moved closer in a low crouch, unseen.

The second forester, whose blonde beard and fair skin seemed to glow in the gloom, crouched down in front of young Much, eyes shining with cruel mirth. 'He looks like a fish, sir!' he crowed. 'A fish on the riverbank, trying not to die.'

The three foresters chuckled. Robin raised his bow, though he could not risk drawing the string back for fear that they would hear it creaking. He only had one shot – one shot to save Much's life.

Still holding his breath, Robin drew back his arrow and let it fly. It covered the distance in half the blink of an eye, slicing through Much's bowstring and freeing him from his accidental noose. As Much fell forward, gasping in great lungfuls of air, Robin flattened himself against his tree.

'Ambush!' cried the big forester. Robin heard the stamp of their footsteps and the swish of their broad blades as they circled warily, searching for their attackers.

A burst of noise sounded from the east. Much was running.

'He's getting away!' cried the blonde Forester. 'After him!'

As the Foresters gave chase, Robin threw up the hood of his cloak and stepped out into the open. 'Don't waste your time with the boy!' he called. 'You'll get a bigger reward for arresting me.'

The foresters stopped and turned, the biggest one taking a step forward as he squinted to see better. He pointed a thick finger at Robin.

'The Hooded Man!' he gasped.

Robin kept his head lowered, knowing the hood would keep his whole face in shadow. 'Indeed,' he replied. 'You're not really going to chase after a young boy when you have the chance to apprehend Robin Hood, are you?'

Realisation dawned on the third forester, whose face was drawn and gaunt. His tunic was absurdly big on him, looking ready to fall over his shoulders and to the ground. Robin could see him dripping with sweat – which was odd, as the October air was chilly. This man did not look well.

The largest forester stepped forward, pointing with his blade. 'The Sheriff will reward us well for capturing you,' he said. 'We can retire from this thankless life chasing bandits.'

The blonde one nudged the gaunt, sweaty forester. 'Especially now those vagabonds have started... biting, eh, Joseph?'

'He got lucky,' said the pale one, in between heaving breaths. 'That's all. And had I not been as ill as I am, I'd have skewered that poacher just now.'

'You may yet skewer Robin Hood,' said the big man.

Robin nodded, eyes on the foresters' broadswords. He slung his bow over his shoulder and drew his own sword.

The big forester grinned. 'That puny thing?' he said. 'My sword can snap that blade in half.'

Robin looked at his weapon. It was true, it was a narrow blade – light, perfect for quick strikes. But his opponent's sword was made for chopping off heads. 'Indeed,' he said. 'It probably can. But you'll never know.'

'And why's that?' asked the Forester.

Robin grinned at his opponent. 'Because a fat brute like you could never catch me.'

The big forester's face reddened as he bared his teeth in anger. He lunged forward, sword raised with deadly intent.

Robin held his blade low, standing his ground as the Forester charged him. At the last moment, he took one step forward, stooped and drove his dropped shoulder safely underneath the deadly sword and into his opponent's gut, the momentum allowing Robin to flip him over his shoulder.

It was a move Robin had perfected from years of sparring with Little John. To the untrained eye, he looked like he possessed unnatural strength. The secret was, you didn't need to be strong to lift a giant off his feet. You just had to be clever.

The blonde Forester and his sickly friend looked at their leader – who was on the ground, out cold – and then at Robin.

'It's true,' said the sickly one. 'Robin Hood does have the strength of ten men!'

'Don't be daft!' said his friend, though he did not look entirely convinced. 'Flank him!' They side-stepped away from each other, taking up positions either side of Robin, keeping their swords trained on him.

Robin kept his own sword held low, biting his

cheeks against a smile. This was just too easy.

The two foresters took cautious steps forward. They paused a moment, the only sound in Sherwood Forest their ragged, nervous breaths. Robin stared straight ahead, not looking at either of them, but keeping both on the edges of his vision. His posture was relaxed – in a fight, being tense and taut slowed you down.

The first thing Robin heard was the singing of the blades as they were pulled back to strike. Then the trampling of dropped twigs either side of him, as the foresters took their first steps forward. Then the *swish* of two swords swinging right at his neck.

Robin dropped into a sitting position, feeling the rush of air almost take the hood off his head. The clang of the foresters' blades bounced off the trees and died away in seconds. As Robin backward rolled into a standing position, he let go of his sword.

By the time Robin was on his feet, the foresters were half-turning away from each other, and towards him. They had closed the gap between themselves to just half a foot, which was what Robin was hoping for.

Robin reached out and took both men by the backs of their heads. He brought their skulls together, the sound of bone knocking bone echoed through the forest. They were out cold before they hit the ground.

Robin picked up his sword and sheathed it. Then he picked up the foresters' swords and set off after Much.

Chapter Four

Robin caught up with Much a mile and a half from their camp. The young Outlaw sat by a tree-trunk, hunched and waiting for his leader. This was how Robin had found the lad five years ago, the day his father, Mark the Miller, had died. He looked as frightened now as he had then.

Mark's home had been a favoured sanctuary for Robin and the Outlaws, a place in which they could hide on their way back to Sherwood from Nottingham. They paid Mark well for his risks, even though he insisted that he would have hid them for free. The day Robin found young Much lost and alone in the forest, he learned that the miller had been betrayed and taken away to the Sheriff's castle. He was threatened with the noose as the Sheriff demanded he betray the Outlaws, and lure them into a trap so the Sheriff could arrest them. Mark refused, and was hung the next day.

Robin never found the traitor. The only way he saw he could do right by Mark was to keep Much close. Now, he looked after the boy like he was his own son.

Robin called out to him. '*Waes hael*, young Much!'

Much, startled enough to reach for his bow as he stood up, saw Robin and half-smiled. 'I gathered it was you who helped me, sir,' he said. 'One day, I hope I can shoot as well as you.'

'One day, you will,' said Robin as he walked past him, clapping him on the shoulder and handing him two of the Foresters blades to carry. 'Come. We will walk together back to camp, free from spying Norman eyes.' But Much did not follow. He stared at the mossy ground.

Robin turned and went to him. 'Do not dwell on this afternoon,' he said. 'The Sheriff and his Norman masters grow eager and desperate. It was only a matter of time before the Foresters started coming this deep into Sherwood. Any one of us could have encountered them.'

'But it was not "any one of us", was it?' Much said, his voice a stifled whisper. Robin saw his teeth clenched in controlled anger. 'I just wish that it wasn't always me who needed rescuing...'

'You're just sixteen,' said Robin, placing a firm hand on Much's shoulder. 'You'll learn. Now, come – let's go home.' Robin Hood lead the way through the forest, and Much followed.

An hour later, Robin and Much emerged through the birch trees into a secret glade. As they set foot in the clearing, sunlight and chilly air embraced them.

Robin led Much across the glade, a slanted-square clearing walled by birch trees. The trees stood like a King's audience, kowtowing before the mighty Major Oak – the grandest tree Robin had ever seen, its trunk almost as thick as a castle turret, and its low branches strong enough to support even Little John. It lorded over them all from the northwest corner of the glade.

Robin and Much weaved in and out of the jumbled rows of tents. Wood smoke from the many fires threw a dull, greyish veil over the glade.

Robin looked over the men as he passed them. Good men, courageous – weapons always in their belts, or on their shoulders. Eyes alert, if tired and weary. The life of an Outlaw was a desperate one – an outlawed man had no home, and no job; he wore the same clothes for most of the year; and if he managed two meals in a day, fate was being kind to him.

As he passed by, returning the grins with smiles of his own, Robin heard the men keeping their spirits up by recounting heroic stories of the Outlaws' defiance, or old Saxon songs from their childhood.

Yes, the life of an Outlaw was desperate. But it was the only life left for these men.

Robin's band numbered nearly sixty. His great friend and mentor, Will Scarlet, worried that there were too many to keep in order; that such a number would grow too rowdy, too boisterous, attracting the attention of the Foresters and revealing the most secret hideout in England.

But Robin Hood had never been able to turn anyone away, not when they came asking for sanctuary. 'If you had refused me,' Robin often said to Will, 'what path would the exiled young Robert of Locksley have walked? Would he have ever become Robin Hood?'

Robin felt a brief pang of loss at memories of his castle, his former life as the son of Byron, the Saxon Earl of Locksley, whose lands were poached by Normans who dreamed up charges of treason. It was then that Robert was outlawed, hunted and eventually driven into Sherwood, where he became known by his Outlaw name – Robin Hood.

How much easier it had been then, and how precarious life was now. In the dead of night, when he would sit alone on sentry duty, staring into a dying fire, Robin wondered what he would do if he could have his time back.

Each night brought a different answer.

Finally, he and Much came to their tents, which had been erected in the shadow of the Major Oak along with those of Robin's most trusted Outlaw companions, who greeted them now – Will Scarlet, their leader and Robin's mentor; the 'bearded mountain' Little John; Friar Tuck, chaplain of Sherwood Forest; and the Butcher, their resident chef.

'My friends!' cried Robin. 'I would have you take a seat, for I have quite the amusing tale to tell.'

As he unhooked his bow and quiver, setting them on the ground beside the bundle of blackened, ashy logs where yesterday evening's fire had burned, Robin caught Much shooting him an anxious look. Robin grinned back and winked to reassure him that he would not be telling 'The Story of How Much the Miller's Son Almost Hung Himself'.

'As you know,' said Robin, 'this morning, I visited the Nottingham fair...'

'...I was too swift, too deadly for the strongman...'

It was twenty minutes later, and Robin was nearing the end of a tiring rendition of the tale of 'Robin Hood and The Strongman', complete with shadow-fighting to fully illustrate his battle against an oaf from York who had challenged any and every man in Nottingham to a fight, proving the 'superiority' of the northerners. Robin's five most trusted Outlaw companions sat around the dead fire, with varying degrees of interest and belief on their faces as he spun his incredible yarn.

Robin was almost breathless as he brought his anecdote to a close, miming his strike with his broken staff to the Strongman's sides, that had hastened the conclusion of their bout. 'His ribs cracked beneath my blows,' he narrated. 'He doubled over, struggling to breathe, sucking at the air like a fish out of the river. And then...'

Robin raised his invisible weapons, but did not mime the final, winning strike. A good storyteller never dictated to his audience, and always let their imagination rule.

'Yes, Robin, sir? And then...?' said Much.

Five pairs of eyes turned on the young Outlaw. There was a shared furrowing of brows among the older men. Will Scarlet simply shook his grey head.

'He hit him over the bonce, Much!' cried Little John, always the first to chide him for being an arrow short of a full quiver.

'Oh!' Much nodded, smiling.

'There's just one thing I simply *have* to know,' said the Butcher, gazing intently at Robin. 'Did you get me the cinnamon I asked for?'

The groan from Little John was like a rumble of thunder as he rose to his full seven-foot. 'I can't bear another rant from the Cook.'

'Call me that again,' said the Butcher, staring after the giant of Sherwood as he lumbered into the forest, 'and you will end up in one of my stews!'

Much, his eyes widening in his young face, chuckled, pointing at where Little John had disappeared among the slanting birch trees. 'Hah! Little John would feed our whole camp for several weeks!'

From between the trees came a stone, hurled with great force, which Much only just managed to duck.

Friar Tuck shook his head, his bald scalp reflecting the sunlight. 'You never learn, do you, lad?'

Robin laughed. 'If only young Much's brain could keep pace with his mouth!'

Robin turned to Will Scarlet, who was himself rising to his feet. His knees cracked, as if protesting his movements. His Lincoln Green hung off his frail old body, just like his saggy skin almost dangled off his bones. The lines of age in his face were so deep, they looked like scars; his voice was as creaky as a tree branch in a storm.

It saddened Robin to see his most trusted Outlaw brother in the autumn of his life. Soon, it would be the winter. How old was Will Scarlet? Robin did not know for sure – Will had never told him.

'What were you doing,' said Will, 'getting into fights at the fair?'

'I was in no danger,' said Robin.

Will shook his head. 'Of course you were!'

'There's really no cinnamon?' It was the Butcher.

Robin and Will ignored him.

'You were there in disguise,' Will continued, 'yet you revealed yourself just so you could show off. Robin, if pride were gold, yours would be enough to make every man in England a lord. It will one day betray you. You said yourself, there were two dozen sergeants there.'

Robin nodded, trying not to grin. There had actually been only four, but he had been creative with the truth. 'Yes, there were,' he said, 'and there could have been two dozen more and they still would not have apprehended me!'

'Maybe,' said Will, the lines around his grey eyes deepening as his face clouded with a wistful sadness. 'But you were reckless to even venture to that fair.

You're still as careless and arrogant as you were when you came here.'

'I haven't been caught,' said Robin. 'And I won't be. Not ever.'

Will Scarlet might have been old, but his hand was still quick. He cuffed Robin round the ear. He was the only man in England who would dare do such a thing. He was also the only man who could get away with it.

'What happens if one day you make a mistake?' he demanded, with his hand held out, palm upwards. Robin knew that his mentor was begging for a good answer. 'If you're a little slow? What becomes of the Nottingham Outlaws if Robin Hood is arrested? What happens if the noose drops over your head?'

'Seriously...' It was the Butcher again, hands on his hips. 'There's no cinnamon?'

Robin tore his gaze from Will Scarlet and looked at the Butcher. 'What were you planning?' he asked. 'What was the big idea for dinner?'

The Butcher shook his head and began stomping away. 'Oh, what's the point?' he wailed. He jabbed an angry finger at Much. 'This one came back with no deer!'

'Oh, stop your whining,' Will growled. 'Surely

we've enough supplies for you to make us a potage.'

The Butcher spun on his heels, his face red with indignity. '"A potage", he says! What do you think this is, Will, a traveller's inn? How dare you ask *me* to make a potage!?' His face still red with rage, the Butcher spat on the grass and marched off.

'Butcher,' Robin called after him, hoping the smile he felt on his face could be not detected in his voice. 'I am sorry!'

The Butcher did not answer. Robin turned back to Will Scarlet, cocking his thumb at the disappearing form of their friend. 'Every day!' he said.

Will did not respond. He gazed at Robin, unblinking, still waiting for an answer.

Robin held his gaze for a long moment, pondering. He was a lot younger than Will and would not have to worry about being slow for many years – if he ever grew slow at all. He was Robin Hood, and he felt like he could keep this up until Kingdom come.

'This will not do,' he said, finally.

Will Scarlet nodded. 'I'm glad you are starting to see reason.'

'I must compensate the Butcher. I will make haste to the river, where I will catch him some fine trout.'

Will's face was in his hands. He growled into his

palms, pulling them away and half-turning towards Friar Tuck, the only Outlaw to have not moved since the conclusion of Robin's tale. He sat, crossed-legged and with his eyes closed, deep in thought – Robin never knew what the thoughts were, but he liked to think they were deep, ponderous and wise. It was comforting to have a Friar in the ranks.

'Good Friar,' said Will, 'I implore you. Talk sense into him.'

Friar Tuck did not even open his eyes. 'Leave me out of it.' That was always his answer. The Friar was the finest of men, and a fierce warrior when he had to be – but he preferred to avoid conflict where he could.

Robin grinned at Will. 'We shall eat well tonight.' And before Will could say anything more, Robin turned to the Friar. 'My wise and noble friend,' he said, 'please gift me with your company as I set about making good on my debt to the Butcher.'

Friar Tuck opened one eye to gaze at Robin. 'Do you mean, you want me to go fishing with you?'

Robin nodded.

Friar Tuck shook his head as he pitched forward to get to his feet. 'Well, just say that, then!'

Chapter Five

'You seek counsel,' said Friar Tuck. 'But not just spiritual – tactical, as well.'

Robin nodded, 'Your perception is almost frightening, Friar.'

He was laying down on George's Bridge, the oak log that was used as a crossing over the River Idle, staring up at a rare, unbroken glade of sky not hidden behind the forest canopy. The afternoon sun beat down on him in gentle waves.

He turned to Friar Tuck, whose gaze was on the flowing waters beneath the log. As always, it was the Friar doing the fishing. Robin never had the patience.

'The Sheriff's Foresters have come deeper into Sherwood than they have ever dared before,' he said. 'Our enemy grows confident.'

'Or desperate,' said the Friar. 'He has been hunting you now for seven years. I'm sure that failure is gnawing at him, somewhat.'

'Either way,' said Robin, 'I fear that our lives as Outlaws will now become more dangerous than ever.'

The Friar flicked his wrists to send the light steel

hook on the end of a line back into the river. He looked solemnly at Robin, unblinking. 'We always knew this was going to happen.'

Robin smiled. 'Are you going to make me *dig* the advice out of you?'

Friar Tuck grinned back at Robin, laying his line down across his ample thigh. 'Sherwood is still your domain. As long as you don't let the Sheriff lure you from the forest, you will be in control of your destiny. Our enemy will doubtless try some dirty tricks – we must be ready for them.'

Robin pushed himself up on to his elbows. 'I dread to think what dirty tricks the Sheriff might try next. Surely we've seen everything he can throw at us?'

Tuck smiled. 'Don't underestimate a desperate man – especially not one with so much foolish pride.'

Robin lay back down and stared up at the sky. 'In a way,' he said, 'I actually admire his persistence. Most people would have given up after so many humiliating defeats.'

'He is loyal to Prince John,' said the Friar. 'And while our good King Richard is away on Crusade, his wicked younger brother holds power. And Prince John wants your head almost as badly as the Sheriff does.'

Robin's smile was grim. 'They will be left wanting.'

'If the Lord wills it,' said the Friar. 'But all the same, I know I'd feel better if the King returned.'

'We can't rely on that, Friar,' said Robin. 'The good people of England are on their own.'

Friar Tuck sighed. 'And that is why our great friend Will is so restless these days. He is going to retire soon, and make you leader of the Outlaws. He wants to be sure that you'll fight not just the good fight, but the smart one too.'

Robin sat up. 'Is that just your way of calling me stupid? Because I'm not afraid to shove a Friar into the River.'

The Friar grinned. 'You haven't the strength.'

Smiling back at him, Robin reached out and hooked an arm around one of the Friar's legs. He pulled up on it and used it to tip Tuck into the river. As Robin leaned forward, laughing, the Friar emerged, coughing and spitting water. 'Well, that confirms it,' said Robin's friend. 'No fish to be caught in there.'

Still laughing, Robin reached down from the bridge. The Friar took it and, before Robin could react, gave it a yank. Robin hit the water with a splash, re-emerging right by the Friar's side.

'A draw,' he spluttered, sweeping his drenched hair from his face.

'Crafty, Robin,' said Tuck. 'Very crafty.'

Robin winked at him. 'You doubted my strength.'

'Aye,' said Tuck. 'I shouldn't have. And after you carry me safely out of this freezing cold river, I will never do it again.'

'I already offered to help you out,' said Robin. 'My reward was a dunking of my own.'

The Friar spread his hands, questioning. 'Was I supposed to let your craftiness go unpunished?'

Robin mirrored the gesture. 'Was I supposed to let your challenge go unanswered?'

Too late, Robin realised he had been outwitted. 'Will you let *this* challenge go unanswered?'

Robin shook his head, smiling. Robin may have been crafty, wily – but he was nothing compared to the Friar. 'Fine,' he said, wading through the water to stand in front of Tuck, who placed his huge hands on Robin's shoulders. Robin reached behind himself to take hold of the Friar's legs, suddenly doubting his ability to piggyback his portly friend. But he couldn't back down now – not after the Friar had challenged him.

'Hurry up,' said the Friar, 'I'm getting chilly.'

Robin half-stepped and half-dragged his feet through the water, Tuck's bulk bearing down on him. He grit his teeth with the effort, feeling his body pitching forward, willing himself not to lose his balance.

If he fell, he would never hear the end of it.

A grunt escaped Robin's lips. He was about five feet from the riverbank. Almost there. He could feel the muddy riverbed clinging more fervently to his feet with every step; he could feel the bend of his knees getting lower and lower. The water, which had began at his chest, was almost up to his chin now.

Finally, he made it, half-turning to drop the Friar on the bank. The holy man crawled away from the water. By the time he raised his head, Friar Tuck was already on his feet and walking away from the bank. Robin held up a hand.

'Some assistance, good Friar,' he called.

The Friar turned round, a wicked gleam in his eyes. 'Surely a strong lad like you needs no assistance.'

As the Friar continued walking back towards the camp, Robin laughed and shook his head.

'Oh, I'll get him for this,' he muttered, as he clambered on to the bank.

Chapter Six

'I can't believe I actually cooked a...'

The Butcher shook his head and shovelled a spoonful of the potage into his mouth, looking as disgusted with the food as he was with its name. The River Idle had offered Robin and the Friar nothing, leaving the Butcher no choice but to cobble together a potage.

He had grumbled all through the cooking; he glared at the pot of boiling green vegetables, chopped his onions and garlic like he was attacking a Nottingham sergeant, and ripped apart bread like it was soggy parchment.

Friar Tuck, who sat near the fire to warm his soaked clothes, raised his bowl. 'It is delicious,' he reassured the Butcher, narrowing his eyes over his bowl at the others, who all sat cross-legged in an uneven circle. The message was clear: *Back me up.*

'Oh, aye,' said Little John, in between mouthfuls. 'Very tasty.'

'I hope we have it for supper tonight too!' said Much.

Will Scarlet offered a smile. 'A triumph, my dear Butcher,' he said.

Robin grunted, stirring his soup with his spoon. 'It could do with some cinnamon.' He laughed as he snapped out a hand to catch the lump of bread aimed straight for his face. The other Outlaws tried not to join in, but they could not resist – even the Butcher's look of annoyance was shredded by a smile.

They all laughed, except for Will, whose watery grey eyes roved over the group like torchlight, gazing at one man, then the next. Robin looked down into his bowl before their eyes met.

He could not imagine life in Sherwood Forest, life as an Outlaw, without Will Scarlet by his side. Robin had learned more from him than from his own father, and valued his counsel even higher than Friar Tuck's. Will's impending retirement forced Robin to ask himself a difficult question: *Can I do this on my own?*

Robin let his own gaze wander over the glade. The rest of his men were also arranged in clusters of six or seven, and were all eating potages made up of varying ingredients, whatever they had picked up on their individual travels. If Much had caught a deer in the forest, the Butcher would have fed everybody in a great feast; but without the deer, everyone stayed in their groups. That had been another stroke of Will's genius – dividing the ever-growing band of free men into smaller companies, each one responsible to a lieutenant, who would report to Will and Robin. It kept the Outlaws organised and stopped them from descending into chaos.

A cry went up from the group sat on the edge of the glade, plucking Robin from his reverie. He was too far away to hear their words, but their tone carried across the camp loud and clear. An intruder had been spotted.

'To arms,' Robin called, 'now!'

Robin and his five companions got to their feet, carelessly setting down their bowls and reaching for their weapons – Robin, his bow and arrow; Will, his long sword with its two ruby studs; Little John, his double-headed axe; Friar Tuck, his staff made from the wood of the Major Oak; Much, his twin short daggers; the Butcher, his spear.

As one, Robin and his friends ran across the glade, weaving in and out of the tents, hopping over fires abandoned as the rest of the Outlaws took up arms. Robin did not have to command them – they rehearsed these ambush scenarios once a week, and the men knew to take up their positions on the borders of the glade, all weapons facing outwards, making sure they were protected from attack from any direction.

Amid his tension, Robin felt a pang of sorrow strike at his heart when he realised that he had left Will Scarlet far behind. How long had he been able to outrun him? There was a time when Robin would strain his leg muscles just to keep up with the man.

Robin drew to a stop beside Lance, the lieutenant who had sent up the call. 'What is it, Lance?' asked Robin, hearing his five companions catch up with him.

'I'm not sure, sir,' said Lance. 'But something moves through the trees.'

'"Something moves through the trees"?' parroted Little John, his voice wheezy from exertion. 'Probably a bird, you skinny numbskull.'

Lance did not rise to the insult. 'This is no bird, sir,' he said.

Robin strung an arrow to his bow and raised it. His eyes narrowed as he looked down the shaft. Behind him, everyone fell silent as they took up position on the edge of the glade, all of them listening hard for the sound of the intruder.

After three seconds, Robin lowered his bow.

'Robin!' hissed Will beside him. 'How many times

must I tell you, stay focused! Do not lower your weapon.'

'Stand down, men!' called Robin, ignoring the exasperation on Will's face. 'This is not an ambush.'

A murmuring rippled through the men. Robin slid the arrow back into his quiver, and slung his bow over his shoulder. He looked at Will. 'Come on, Will,' he said, 'use your nose. When was the last time you met a Norman soldier who wore the scent of lavender?'

'You are a jumpy lot,' came a voice from high in the trees. A soft, lilting voice – one Robin knew well. 'All this fuss over one measly intruder.'

The Outlaws glanced heavenward. Leaves rustled and branches broke as a lithe woman burst into the glade, so fast she was little more than a blur of Lincoln Green as she dropped from the trees, landing in a neat, cat-like crouch before the Outlaws.

She was as tall as Robin, her frame slender and sleek, save for the hardened muscles at her arms and shoulders, and her strong legs – the result of fierce fighting, hard running and long horse rides. She stood with a wide, masculine stance, one hand on the sword at her left hip. Her skin was pale and her hair was a thicket of red curls, tumbling down the sides of her beautiful face like a waterfall.

Another murmur, more excited than the last, went round the glade again, the lady's name passed from Outlaw to Outlaw like a gift.

'The Lady Marian!'

All around the camp, the men threw up a hearty cheer, which Marian returned with a smile and half-bow.

Robin felt a matching smile on his own face for a second, before a more serious thought chased it away. Marian was a Baron's daughter who had chosen exile over a forced betrothal to Prince John, absconding into the Forest with her own dowry. Now, she led the freewomen of Nottingham just as Robin led the freemen – but she was very far from her own camp, which was in the south of the forest.

Only the gravest of situations would have prompted Marian to ignore the rule that she and Robin had made several years before – that their camps would remain as separate and independent as possible; that Nottingham's Sheriff may well crush one band of Outlaws, but never both.

Marian, as always, knew exactly what Robin was thinking. Her smile fell away, and she eyed Robin and Will with a sombre expression. 'I need to talk to you – alone.'

'Trouble brews in Nottingham,' said Marian. 'Trouble the like of which we have never known.'

They were sat around a fire in the shadow of the Major Oak. Marian's deep brown eyes gazed at Robin over the tip of the flames. Will, Little John, Friar Tuck, Much and the Butcher were scattered around them. Will listened intently to Marian's words, as did John and Tuck. Much's mind seemed to wander. The Butcher was tasting the leftover potage, wearing an expression of surprised contentment.

'What do you mean?' Robin asked Marian.

'A plague, Robin,' she replied. 'A plague has fallen on the city.'

Little John rose to his feet with alarming speed for a man his size. 'What?'

Robin, who was nearest to him, took a handful of John's cloak and tugged on it, trying to get him to sit down. 'Be calm, John,' he said. 'Let us hear the lady out.'

'But, Robin, my *family*...'

Robin regarded his giant friend, his expression softening with sympathy. In becoming an Outlaw, Little John had left behind in Nottingham a loyal wife and young son.

'Surely word would have reached us,' Will pointed

out, voicing Robin's immediate thought. 'The gates would have been closed to travellers, pits would have been dug for the dead. We would have heard about a plague.'

'He's right,' said Robin. 'I visited the fair this morning, there seemed no sign of any plague. But...' All eyes turned to Robin. He was remembering something else – that happened *after* the fair.

'What?' asked Little John, his face desperate.

'I encountered some foresters on my way back,' said Robin. 'And one of them looked gravely ill.'

Marian sighed, nodding sadly. 'Did he have any strange wounds?' she asked.

Robin shook his head. 'Not that I saw... But his companions made a joke about him being bitten by someone.'

Marian's eyes dropped.

'I think,' said Robin, 'that you had better tell us your story, my lady.'

And so Marian told Robin and his most trusted companions her story – a story so grave, and odd, even Much and the Butcher started paying attention again.

'We made the short journey to Nottingham,' she

said. 'Three of us – myself, and my Outlaw sisters, Jeanette and Eleanor. They wanted to deliver to their parents a few silver pennies so that they might buy warmer clothes for the coming winter months.'

Robin saw Marian's eyes fill with tears that she blinked away.

'But we never made it to their home,' she said. 'A short way into Nottingham, we happened upon a fallen yeomen. It was a chilly day, but he was writhing on the ground and tearing at his clothes, shouting about a "burning". We could see his skin was red like it had been scalded by boiled water, and that sweat almost gushed from his face.

'The three of us feared that he carried some sort of plague, and I'm ashamed to say we kept our distance – though it seemed that we could escape the sight of him, but not the sound. His cries...'

Marian's eyes were fixed on the fire. Robin could see the reflected flames dancing in the deep brown lakes that shone with grief and regret.

'From our position further down the street,' Marian continued, 'we saw the man rip off his clothes. There were deep scratches on his chest, probably from where he had clawed at himself. He crawled slowly, panting as though he couldn't breathe. Throughout it all, he said two words over and over again. "It burns."'

Marian let that statement hang in the air. Robin stared into the fire, hoping for a smart thought – a leader's thought – to come to mind. But his head was empty.

'Did no one go to the man's aid?' asked Will.

Marian shook her head. 'No one,' she said. 'Except town sergeants.'

Robin snorted. 'I wouldn't have expected them to be brave enough to help.'

'That's the thing,' said Marian. 'I don't think they did help.'

Robin shared a confused look with Will as another silence descended over the group, broken only by Little John's deep breathing. Robin knew his friend was trying to keep calm and keep his anger in check. He would not succeed for long.

'If they didn't help,' said Friar Tuck, 'what did they do?'

'I don't know exactly,' said Marian. 'Four of them came, fully-armoured. They took a limb each and dragged him away. The three of us followed as quietly as we could. We saw the sergeants place the sickly man in a cart, and cover him up with a heavy blanket. We followed them some more, but I thought it too risky.'

'Any idea where they went?' asked Robin.

'I can only guess,' replied Marian. 'But it was in the direction of the Sheriff's castle. We went into the town. Like you at the fair, Robin, we saw no sign of panic – everything seemed quite normal. Except for a few closed-up shops. But I know what I saw – there is a plague brewing in Nottingham.'

'To Nottingham!' John cried, throwing up his mighty hands. 'All of us – every Outlaw, man and woman.'

Robin jumped to his feet. 'My good fellow, please try to be calm.'

'Calm?' bellowed the giant. 'How can I be calm? My wife and son…' He broke off, unable to finish his sentence. Being neither a father nor husband, Robin could not imagine what was going through Little John's mind. But he needed his biggest, strongest Outlaw composed, for his shouts had reverberated through the entire glade and drawn anxious glances in their direction.

'For once, Robin talks sense,' said Will, as he forced himself to his feet, which prompted everyone else around the fire to rise. Marian, right beside the old Outlaw, half-gestured to assist him, but Will waved her away. 'We cannot be reckless.'

Much gasped. 'Will, we can't abandon an Outlaw Brother's family.'

'We won't,' said Will. 'But we must be careful – we cannot just ride into Nottingham headfirst. Not when we don't know what dangers lie in wait there.'

'I don't care,' said Little John. 'I will go alone if no one else will!'

Robin gazed up at the sky, the position of the sun. 'Two hours before sunset,' he commented. 'Enough time for us to reach the gates of Nottingham, if we ride hard. We will go in disguise, and speak to no one. Little John will find his family. If there's time, we will leave the town. If not, we will stay in Nottingham and leave at first light. We can do this.'

Robin surveyed his gathered men, and Marian. They all nodded back at him, their eyes showing some fear, but even more determination.

Will Scarlet's eyes narrowed. 'On your head be it, Robin,' he said.

Robin regarded the others still standing by the fire. 'Go make ready,' he told them, his voice not hiding his true meaning: *Leave Will and I in peace.*

Robin and Will looked at each other for a long moment, Robin feeling his throat tighten at what he was about to say. 'I want you to stay here.'

Will blinked in surprise. 'What?'

Robin placed a hand on Will's shoulder. 'I don't want you with us. It's too dangerous.'

'How dare you speak to me—'

'Will...' Robin tightened his grip on the old man's shoulder. 'You have been like a father to me since I was first Outlawed. You taught me archery and swordsmanship. You made Robert of Locksley into Robin Hood. You are the bravest man I have ever known. But you are also an old man now – and you can't run as fast as you used to. You know that. You must leave this to us.'

With a smile, Will nodded, and mirrored Robin's affectionate gesture. 'Thank you,' he said.

'What for?' asked Robin.

'Proving to me that you can make a leader's choices,' said Will. 'Telling your mentor to stay at home cannot have been easy.'

Robin laughed. 'It wasn't.'

Still smiling, Will stepped away from Robin and stooped to pick up his sword. 'But I'm still going to Nottingham.'

Robin shook his head. 'Will, I—'

Will turned back to Robin as he strapped his jewelled sword to his waist. 'Let me have a final day as an Outlaw. When we return to Sherwood, I'll retire.' With a smile, Will held out his hand. 'One last ride?'

Robin thought about it for a few seconds. Would Will's age and lack of speed be a burden to them? Or would his cool head and experience be an advantage?

Robin made his decision. He clasped Will's hand. 'One last ride.'

Chapter Seven

Robin drew his group to a stop when he saw the tower of St Mary's church in the distance, peering over the stone walls of the city like a watchful eye on approaching travellers. He was at the head of the group, one hand full of the reins of the carthorse they had stolen from Godfrey, that Friar Tuck had named Fury.

Robin looked across Fury's snout at Will Scarlet. The Outlaws wore heavy red cloaks instead of their usual Lincoln Green, and wide-brimmed hats to hide their faces from any sergeants who might recognise them. Whenever they entered Nottingham the Outlaws passed themselves off as traveller sellers from the West Country, and no one gave them a second glance.

'Everyone ready?' he asked.

There were nods and grunts of assent. Robin turned round to face Much, who stood with Little John behind the cart. John's agitation was almost wafting off him like a bad smell, while Much's shoulders were hunched and his eyes wide.

'Much,' said Robin, 'check the cart one more time.'

Much leaned forward, his slender hand patting the thick blanket of straw that lined the cart. 'They're well hidden, Robin,' he said.

He was referring to the Outlaws' weapons, which were buried beneath the straw, as well as the sacks of grain – and money – that Robin and John had claimed from the tax collector in the forest. The group looked no more serious and threatening than a bunch of merchants who had had a good day's trading and were looking to sell the last of their stock in Nottingham.

Robin nodded. 'Good. Let's hurry to the gates. We don't have much time.'

The group moved along again, their cart's steel-rimmed wheels following deep tracks in the road that had already taken a battering from countless hooves, wheels and feet.

A short way from the gate, the road crossed a shallow, dank brook. 'Mind your back, good sir,' Robin called, in a West Country accent, startling a townsman who was stooped over the muddy bank, emptying a sack of rubbish into the water. Robin couldn't see what the rubbish was, but it smelled foul. Behind him, he heard Much dry-heave, and felt him push at the back of the cart to get it moving faster.

The group fell into line behind another man, as the weak, fading sun threw long shadows of the gatehouse over them. A stone archway bound two tall towers together. As he always did, Robin mentally counted off the sergeants he could see. There were seven visible – three checking those entering the city, and four perched on the walls, lazily holding crossbows as they watched the road.

'What's your business here?' asked one of the sergeants on the ground. He eyed them with none of the dubiousness Robin would have expected him to have at a group of travellers turning up so close to the ringing of the Curfew Bell.

'Just selling the last of our grain, sergeant,' said Robin, in his fake accent.

The sergeant looked them over one more time. Robin could tell, from the flickering of his eyes, that he was counting them off. He mouthed the word 'Seven' to himself.

Finally, the sergeant nodded, lips forming a thin smile. 'Right,' he said, 'pay your toll and sell your stock, quick as you can. Welcome to Nottingham.'

Robin bowed his thanks to the sergeant, stealing a glance at Will under the brim of his hat. The older Outlaw's expression told Robin he was king the same thing as he was. *That was odd.* The Nottingham guards were usually strict on granting travellers entry this close to nightfall. Robin had expected to be questioned, maybe even turned away and left to find another way in. But this guard offered no resistance. He hadn't even looked inside their cart.

The Outlaws made their way past the sergeant and through the Nottingham gate and out into the main square. The smell of horse manure, dirty straw and earth, and the sound of late-day trading, crashed around like chaotic ocean waves as they made their way against the tide of travelling traders leaving the town at the end of the day.

'Right,' said Robin, keeping up the fake accent to be on the safe side. He looked back over the cart at the others. 'We'll walk around a bit, so we don't look suspicious. Little John will then make his way to his family's house, while the rest of us find a quiet spot where we can sit and hide the grain and the money. I'll leave word with some friends that it is to be found and the money returned in the morning. The plan is to meet at the gate as the Curfew Bell rings. Everyone understand?'

'Aye,' said Little John, using his own voice. 'But

let's hurry it along, Robin.'

'I'm trying, John,' Robin replied, 'but any faster, and I'll be running people over.'

'So run 'em over,' Little John growled. Robin couldn't chide him for his tone.

Robin's gaze fell on the gate. Three sergeants were dragging it closed. *That's odd*, thought Robin

'Did anyone hear the Curfew Bell?' he asked.

There was a short flurry of shaken heads, glances cast back towards the gate. Marian looked back at Robin. 'Why have they closed the—'

Robin felt the cart lurch, the momentum making him stumble. John was pushing them forward faster. 'We can worry about that when it's time to get out,' he said.

They turned right onto Baker's Lane. The cobbled road was barely visible beneath the mass of bodies gathered round every stall. The sound of haggling and bartering as customers challenged bakers to bring down the price on the end-of-day, nearly stale stock was like a sea tide, coming in waves.

Robin quickened his pace at another lurch of the cart. Little John was getting more and more impatient every time the cart slowed. As they passed the first turning off Baker's Lane on to Tanner's Hill and out of sight of the sergeants at the gate, he broke from their group.

'Watch it, you big oaf!' cried a tanner, whose efforts to close up for the day had been interrupted when Little John ran into him.

Robin watched Little John barrel past tanner and customer alike. 'He's going to be noticed by the sergeants before he gets anywhere near his house,' said Robin. 'Much, Friar – catch him and look after him.'

Much and Friar Tuck took off, weaving their way through the crowd after Little John, who had already disappeared around a corner and down another street.

Robin, Will, Marian and the Butcher pushed on through Baker's Lane, finding an inn, where they tethered Fury.

'Will we leave our weapons?' asked Will, raising his voice to be heard over the tuneless ballad sung by drunk men inside the inn.

Robin pondered, thinking aloud. 'I don't like it, but I think we have to. We're dressed as travellers, and travellers with weapons are asked questions.'

'Can't we take the cart to John's house?' asked Marian.

Robin shook his head. 'We'll be too slow and

conspicuous,' he replied. He looked northwards. The Sheriff's castle was just visible above the jumble of low roofs in the town, the windows in the turrets like the dark, cruel eyes of the Sheriff himself, peering at the people, watching them. Robin had never seen the inside of the Sheriff's castle. He did not want that to change.

'Yes,' he said. 'We'll leave the weapons and the cart. One of us should stay behind to look after it.'

A silence fell on the remaining Outlaws, none of whom were keen to volunteer. After a moment, Robin clapped the Butcher on the shoulder. 'Try not to fall asleep,' he said.

Robin, Will and Marian turned and walked away, leaving the Butcher behind, looking as incredulous as if he had just been asked to make an all-vegetable potage.

It took them ten minutes to work their way through the crowded market streets into the quieter residential quarter. Dirty roads meandered in and out of wooden shacks and wattle and daub huts. Robin could see that the road they now walked was not one the town rakers paid much attention to, judging by the crushed leaves and horse dung clogging the central gutters.

He pointed when he saw Much and Friar Tuck at the end of the deserted street, outside Little John's house – a narrow, wooden hovel, that looked barely big enough to accommodate their friend.

By the time he, Marian and Will reached the hut, Robin felt anxiety tingling in his gut – would they have enough time to get back to their inn before curfew? He did not fancy engaging the Sheriff's soldiers at night and unarmed.

But his stomach dropped when he saw the anguished expressions on Much and Tuck's faces. The Friar's eyes were closed, his palms together in prayer; Much sat against the hut, hands on his head as he wept.

Robin felt Marian clutch at his arm. 'Are we too late?' she gasped.

Robin didn't answer. Only a few people seemed to have been affected – and it would be terrible luck if John's family was among them. 'What is it?' Robin asked Tuck.

The Friar opened his eyes and brought his hands down. His bewildered face turned Robin's blood to ice. 'I do not know,' he said. 'This is like nothing I have ever seen before. Like nothing I have ever read about. Nothing I...' The Friar shook his head, and resumed his prayer.

Robin looked from the Friar to Marian and Will, who stood rooted to the spot ten feet away from the house. Robin gestured for them to stay back.

As he approached the door, he caught Much's eye and the young lad's face crumpled as a whimper escaped his lips. If Robin wasn't fearful of what he might find within the hovel before, he was now.

Robin forced himself to look inside.

Chapter Eight

The first thing Robin noticed was the stench of death – rotten, putrid and cloying – mixed with the dull iron smell of blood. He wiped his watering eyes with his sleeve.

Little John sat on a stool in the centre of the room, his massive bulk almost blocking out the light of a dying beeswax candle on a shelf in the far corner. John cradled his five year old son, Peter, in his arms. The boy was curled up in a ball, his skin red and shining with sweat; his face was covered in hideous boils that trailed down his cheeks. His breath came in shallow whimpers, and at each one Little John winced and held him tighter. 'It'll be alright, my boy,' said the big man, over and over again.

'The man did this, Father,' said Peter, spit spraying from his lips as Little John rocked him like a sleepless baby. 'The man with the bleeding eye and the lumps on his face. He scratched me and Mama.'

The boy wriggled in John's embrace and extended his arm, showing three deep gashes running from wrist to elbow. 'It burns,' said Peter. 'It burns on the inside. It burns everywhere. Make it go away, Father.'

'It'll be alright,' Little John repeated. 'I promise…'

Robin leaned on the doorframe to steady himself, his eyes watering as much with grief as from the unbearable air. He tore his eyes away from John and his son, his gaze falling on the inert body of John's wife, Ruth, face down in a widening puddle of thick black sludge that Robin realised was the source of the smell. Specks and slithers of it smeared Ruth's lips and drained from her mouth. Her face was decorated with hideous boils.

Robin turned to Friar Tuck. 'Please, Friar,' he said, 'think hard. Is there no record of such an illness in any book you have read?'

Friar Tuck shook his head. 'Robin, this is like nothing I have read about. Absolutely nothing.'

Robin slapped the doorframe in frustration. There was no known cure for the plague. The only thing they could do was escape the city before they too were infected.

And that meant that there was no hope for Little John's wife and son.

Robin crouched in the doorway, and took a deep breath – which he instantly regretted. 'John,' he said, coughing his lungs clear of the death stench. 'There is nothing we can do. We must—'

'I'm not leaving him alone,' said Little John. 'Not until—'

Peter sat bolt upright, with a speed that made Little John almost stand up in surprise.

'Peter? Oh, no! No!' cried Little John as he wrestled with his writhing son, whose head bobbed forward, as though about to be sick.

'John, he—' Robin said.

Peter's mouth opened so wide it looked like his face was tearing itself in half as a geyser of black bile erupted. It arced across the shack and splattered against the opposite wall. As he scrambled to his feet, Robin was dimly aware of the pungent substance coating Peter's mother, turning her white gown as black as a winter's night.

Peter's body was wracked by powerful convulsions that ripped him free from John's embrace. The boy fell on to his hands and knees, crawling blindly.

As John reached towards his son, Robin strode into the room and took two handfuls of John's tunic. 'We must go!' Robin cried. 'Now!'

Little John fought back for a moment, but soon his grief left him limp. Robin managed to drag him out on to the street. Night was falling over Nottingham.

He noticed that no one had dared venture out to help. He could not blame them.

'Much,' Robin cried, 'close the door!'

As Much did as he was told, Robin wrapped his arms around Little John and held him on the ground. Friar Tuck knelt down next to them and almost shouted his prayers.

Marian cradled John's head as he sobbed; Will Scarlet stood over them, looking at Robin with the same helpless expression as Robin felt on his own face.

Much sat with his back against the shack door. But though the door hid the awful sights, it did not block the sounds of Peter expelling bile from his guts, the wretches and hacks of his body, the slap of it hitting the floor.

After what seemed like an age, Peter fell silent, and Robin guessed the boy had mercifully died. Friar Tuck stood up, still muttering in Latin. He made the sign of the cross in the direction of Little John's house; then he thought for a moment, and made a wide circle, aiming air crucifixes at each house.

The Outlaws sat or stood in the middle of the road, their grief-stricken breaths and Little John's exhausted sobs the only sound.

'We must not linger,' said Will Scarlet, walking towards Much. 'It will soon be curfew – we must retire to the inn, and leave Nottingham at first light.' The old man reached down to grab Much by the shoulder. 'Up you get, there's a good la—'

A hand punched through the door by Much's face. Shards of wood flew in all directions as Much dived aside. Will recoiled with a grunt of shock.

'Ruth!' cried Little John, pushing Marian and Robin aside as he got to his feet. 'She's still alive!'

Robin looked at the hand. The skin was pale – the flesh soft, almost papery. As the hand drew back into the house, the skin snagged on the jagged edge of the hole, peeling off the bone like a skin glove. It fell to the ground where Much had been sitting a moment before.

Then, whatever was inside the house punched a second time, and the whole door flew into the street.

Chapter Nine

Little John stopped several paces from his house. 'I saw my Ruth die,' he mumbled. 'How is this possible?'

The figure in the shattered doorway certainly looked like Ruth, but all the traces of the kindly woman Robin had known were gone. Its gown and hair dripped with black sludge and the bones of its right hand were completely exposed, the flesh torn off halfway up its forearm. Its pallid, boil-covered face was set in a snarl, its cheeks almost caving inwards. Its nose flared in hungry snorts and grunts as it turned to face the Outlaws. It moved slowly, but as deliberately as a predator.

Robin felt bile rise in his throat, and heard Marian gasp: 'Oh, my Lord!' The fiend's left eye wept thin tears of blood that split into two when they struck the boils, the red trails like rambling tree roots down one cheek. Its right eye seemed clouded with a dull, greyish film. Blood and drool dribbled over its slack bottom lip, and the only sound it made was a wet snarl.

The breeze carried the stench of the fiend – a stench that turned Robin's stomach over.

'The dead walk!' cried Friar Tuck. 'They rise as Undead! My Lord God, is this the end of all things? Is this the Day of—' Friar Tuck's words rose to a shriek as the Undead Ruth sprang forwards, hands clawing at the air.

'Run!' Robin shouted.

The Outlaws turned and fled the scrabbling creature. Robin didn't need to look back to know that it was close – he could almost taste death in his mouth, and wished he'd not left their weapons behind.

'To the gate!' Robin called, grabbing John's sleeve in an effort to speed him up. Marian and Much streaked ahead, and behind him Friar Tuck was scampering as fast as his fat legs would carry him.

'*Argh!*'

Robin turned without stopping, almost losing his balance and scraping his hands on the beaten-earth road. 'Oh no...'

Will Scarlet's age had caught up with him.

The old Outlaw was lying face down in the road, with the fiend-Ruth clinging to his back. Will desperately tried to crawl free, his eyes wide with fear as his fingers dug for purchase. He threw back his elbow, slamming it into the Undead lady's face.

But it did not let go.

With a desperate cry, Will kicked his legs, trying to push himself clear.

But it did not let go.

Robin swung his boot at the fiend's head, sending it tumbling over to one side.

But it did not let go.

The fiend dragged Will with it, man and moving corpse rolling across the road. Will drove his elbow into its ribs once, twice, three times.

But it did not let go.

Robin picked up a piece of timber from the broken door and plunged it down into the fiend's face. He felt its skull cave in; he yanked the wood free to reveal a sunken crater between its eyes and mouth.

But it did not let go.

As Robin raised the wood for another strike, he saw the fiend's mouth open and its teeth clamp down on Will's neck, biting through his shaggy grey hair and sending out a spray of blood that splashed Robin's knees. Will's eyes widened with pain, his mouth opening to cry out but the sound was stolen away by the pure shock of what had happened.

Robin swung the jagged piece of wood like an axe at

the fiend's skull, over and over again; each strike made a bigger dent until clumps of what was once Ruth's brain burst and sprayed free. The fiend was finally still, its grip on Will loosening. Robin used the lump of wood – dripping blood, flesh and brain, and studded with shards of bone – to work Will free of the fiend's clutches.

As Robin reached down to help Will to his feet, the old Outlaw shoved him back. Robin fell into the sturdy frame of Little John, who braced him.

'Will!' Robin gasped. 'Let us help you—'

'No use,' said Will, with a bitter laugh. 'There's no use, Robin. Fate has a sense of cruel humour this day. "One last ride" indeed.'

Will crawled back from the fiend and came to a stop a few feet away, on his knees as if in prayer. His head hung forward, and Robin could see blood streaming from the hole in his neck.

'Will, we must go,' said Robin. 'We must get out of this cursed town.'

'Yes, you must,' said Will, 'and you must leave me here.'

Robin stepped towards Will, but the old Outlaw flashed him a look so fierce Robin became still even before he spoke.

'Do as I say, for once!' Will shouted. 'Get out of Nottingham. Raise the alarm, and take as many people with you as you can. And don't come back – not ever.'

'But Will, I don't understand,' said Robin.

Will Scarlet gently raised a hand to the wound in his neck. 'It burns, Robin,' he said. 'It burns on the inside.'

'No…' Robin breathed, shaking his head. 'No…'

'*Yes*,' said Will, raising his head to look at Robin, his eyes showing bitter amusement at his bad luck. 'I think poor Ruth passed her Plague to me, through her bite. I am infected… You must get away from me, and quickly. This infection is going to kill me… I might become like Ruth… I might attack you…'

Robin ran his hands through his hair, holding on to his head as if to stop it bursting. He felt anguish like a rusty blade lodged in his chest.

'Good God, no!' cried Little John. He was looking back up the road, towards his house.

Peter was crawling out through the doorway. Except he wasn't Peter anymore.

And he wasn't the only one.

Door after door all the way up the street was forced open. They clattered to the ground, flipping and tumbling, breaking apart as they collided with each other.

Fiend after fiend stumbled out of the dwellings and into the road on legs that barely seemed to work. As one, they turned in the direction of the stunned Outlaws, their faces set in shared snarls of ravenous, cannibalistic intent.

'What is happening?' Robin breathed. 'How is this possible?'

Will looked over his shoulder, then back at his Outlaw brothers for the last time. He struggled to his feet and reached for the lump of wood Robin held. 'I'll hold them off for as long as I can. Raise the alarm – get the people out. Otherwise everyone in the town will be end up like these creatures. Do it!'

Will turned and ran towards the fiends. The old Outlaw swung the wood, hitting skulls and jaws, jabbing it into chests, not caring for how many times he was scratched by flailing Undead hands.

As Will disappeared among the writhing mass of corpses, Robin tore his eyes away, seeing Friar Tuck gazing to the sky, as if Heaven would answer his questions.

Robin led his group at a trot back down the street, keeping his eyes peeled for any more fiends. 'Everyone gather themselves,' he said. 'Much, Marian, you're the fastest on foot. Go to the inn, find the Butcher and have him bring the cart back to the main gate. We'll meet you there. Tell everyone that you pass that they must leave Nottingham, right now. Tell them, to stay means death – *worse* than death!'

'But the gate is closed,' said Much, wiping his nose with the back of his hand, his eyes as red as a fiend's. 'How will we get past the sergeants?'

'We'll get past them,' Robin said. 'Whatever it takes. Go!'

Marian set a brisk pace through the streets and Much followed.

Robin addressed Little John and Friar Tuck. 'We make for the gate, and we make as much noise as we can. And we get that gate open…one way or another.'

Chapter Ten

The three Outlaws made a chaotic course through the town. They lobbed stones at front doors, and bellowed the word 'Plague!' over and over again.

'Everyone make for the gate!' Robin hollered as he barrelled down the last residential road before turning on to Silk Street.

He skidded to a stop in the middle of the road. No one was moving – the merchants packing up for the day simply looked at the three men with confused expressions.

'You must listen to me,' said Robin. 'A plague has fallen on the town. Everyone must leave if they wish to live.' A few of the sellers looked uneasily at each other, but still no one moved. 'To stay is to die,' Robin shouted. 'And die in the most awful of ways. Please, listen to me.'

A murmuring moved through the merchants.

'He's mad!' said one.

'Probably drunk!' said another.

Robin shot an anxious glance at Friar Tuck – how were they going to convince people to flee?

'Get away, you drunkard,' said one of the merchants. 'Stop causing trouble.'

'I swear to you, I'm not making—'

'*Argh!*'

Everyone looked towards the blood-curdling scream. A woman had fallen on to the dirty cobbles. An Undead man was ripping at her face. Robin almost wretched when he saw the fiend swipe off a handful of the woman's cheek, then force it into its mouth.

They eat flesh, he thought, feeling sick.

A frightened murmur went through the merchants.

Friar Tuck took a step forward to help the woman, but Robin held him back.

'We cannot save her,' he said. 'We must run. They are coming.'

'What is it?' shouted one of the sellers, a tall man stepping numbly into the street, wide eyes fixed on the mauling further down. 'What is that thing?'

'It's the plague,' said Robin. 'It is what will happen to everyone if we don't leave Nottingham right now! To the gates!'

At last, the merchants listened. They fled, running along towards the main square. The three Outlaws joined them, Robin's cries of 'Plague!' scorching his throat until he was almost hoarse.

They were four streets from the main square. Four streets from meeting Marian, the Butcher and Much at the gate, where they would be reunited with their weapons. Robin risked a glance behind him as he turned off Silk Street. He paused at the corner, the fleeing merchants streak away to his right...and half a dozen more Undead rushing towards him on his left.

'Someone's down there,' said the Sheriff, staring through a window in his Great Hall, at the town. The faint sound of chaos drifted up to him from the streets below. 'Someone is causing a panic. And I can guess who it is...' He slapped the stone wall. 'Robin Hood! It has to be – every bad day I've ever had has been that Outlaw's fault.'

'Oh dear, oh dear, oh dear,' said Mother Maudlin in that teasing, taunting voice of hers, as she walked towards him across the Hall, her steps seeming to leave the thick straw beneath her feet eerily undisturbed. The Sheriff's blood to ice; fear and hatred stopped him from looking her in the eye.

'What if everyone escapes, Sheriff?' she asked. 'What if you can't deliver to Prince John all the people of Nottingham, like you promised. He'll be angry. Oh, yes, he will. Why can't you control your town?'

'Why does your devilish magic not work on people?' the Sheriff countered.

The Witch stopped for just a moment, taken by surprise. 'That's...not how it works,' she said.

The Sheriff almost smiled at her evasive answer.

'But anyway,' Mother Maudlin continued, 'you should not be worrying about me. You should be worrying about not breaking your promise to the Prince.'

The Sheriff nodded and looked back out of the window. He could see people running down the streets, all in the same direction – towards the main gate. He could hear the chaotic cries and wordless yells.

There was only one thing for it.

Even though they ran with the tide of people, progress was slow as the three Outlaws emerged into the main square. Most made for the gate. Some sought sanctuary in St. Mary's.

As Robin, John and Tuck joined the throng trying to leave through the gate, the air filled with panicked cries and desperate shouts. Hands clutched and clawed. A tall man to Robin's left took two handfuls of his cloak and practically screamed: 'Is it true? Do the dead walk among us?'

Before Robin could answer, a woman's voice shrieked: I saw them!' Robin looked and saw a lady holding a crying toddler above her head to protect him from the crush. 'Horrible, they were,' she went on. 'Their skin's rotted off like a corpse, and their eyes are bleeding.'

Robin felt his stomach turn again. How many were there? 'We must all get out,' he said. 'Just keep moving forward.'

'But we've stopped,' said the woman. 'What if they don't open the gates?'

'We're trapped,' said the man. 'We're all going to die!' He let go of Robin and flung himself at the people in front of him. 'Move!' he yelled. 'Come on!'

'Good fellow,' said Robin, reaching for him. 'You must try to remain calm. We can force open the gate, but we need to—'

'Out of my way!' the man hollered, aiming a wild punch at the back of an elderly woman in front of him. Before Robin could react, two men turned to accost the first, who threw his head forward and knocked one of them out cold, before the other wrapped him in a bear hug.

'I don't want to die!' cried the man. 'Let us out!'

Robin looked over the crowd, towards the gate. A squad of sergeants jabbed their spears at the people trying to pass them. Crossbowmen on the walls had their weapons raised, ready to shoot. The people arriving at the back of the crowd were creating a surge, which edged those on the front line closer to the points of the sergeants' spears.

Robin was squashed between John and Tuck, unable to move his arms or legs.

'This is hopeless,' said John. 'We're never going to get out of here.'

'Yes, we will,' Robin insisted. 'We outnumber the sergeants. Soon, they will be overrun. Besides, when they see the Undead, they will surely let us out – they'll want to escape as well.'

Three harsh bugle notes rang out across the mayhem.

'Oh no,' said Robin, his heart in his mouth at the sound of the hideous three-note bugle blast, piercing through the sound of chaos at the gate. It came from the Sheriff's castle. And that meant only one thing.

'More sergeants are coming!'

Dozens of mounted sergeants appeared, their armoured heads bobbing above the writhing bodies of the civilians all making for the gate. As they galloped down the cobbled streets, they used the shafts of their spears to knock people aside. Any who fell were trampled.

'They don't look like they're here to help,' said Tuck.

'No, they don't,' said Robin. 'Perhaps they haven't seen the Undead yet and think this is a riot.' Then he remembered Marian's tale about the sergeants taking a dying man to the Sheriff's castle. But what did it *mean*?

Robin forced his way back through the crowd, away from the gate. Little John and Friar Tuck used their bulk to create as much space as they could, but it was still like walking against a tidal wave.

They broke from the crowd with collective sighs, just as Marian and the Butcher led the carthorse towards them from the direction of the inn. Much trotted after them, panic turning his face red. More people were streaming past them, joining the crowd as it battered the town gates.

Robin turned to see sergeants gallop along either side of the crush, thrusting out the shafts of their spears. Within seconds, they had joined the guards at the gates. Their horses reared and kicked at the people in front, driving them back.

Robin looked up a street and saw a group of Undead leap on a man, drag him down and begin to feed. He glanced up at the crossbowman on the walls. *Now they will open the gate and let us out*, Robin thought. *When they see what we are all running from*. But the crossbowman just watched impassively.

'We must find another way out,' said Marian.

Robin went to the cart and retrieved his bow. Next to it was Will Scarlet's long sword. He picked up both, slinging his bow and quiver over his shoulders, and strapping Will's sword around his waist. 'There is no time,' Robin told her. 'The Undead will be upon these people soon and then it will all be over.'

Marian eyed his weapons dubiously. 'What are you going to do?'

Robin said nothing. He looked over her shoulder towards the Nottingham gate and heard the desperate calls of the civilians. A sergeant stabbed someone and the pleading of the crowd grew into an angry, communal bellow – all words fell away into a blanket of dull noise.

Anarchy had fallen on Nottingham.

Robin reached into his quiver and cast his Outlaws a firm glance. 'Be ready,' he said.

'Right,' said Much, using his daggers to cut the

rope tethering Fury to their cart. Freed, Fury nuzzled Much as if in gratitude.

Friar Tuck climbed into the saddle. 'I'll lead,' he said.

'Good luck, Friar,' said Robin.

Ahead, more sergeants on foot had arrived to pile into the crowd, swinging staffs and swords, pushing with their shields in an effort to disperse them.

Robin stepped forward, raising his bow. He found his target – a tall captain in charge of the men protecting the gate. He was well armoured – chain-mail, heavy gauntlets, kite-shaped shield on his left arm, and a helmet.

But his helmet did not protect his whole face – not from an archer as skilled as Robin Hood.

Robin took a deep breath. *The sergeant is trapping people in this cursed town*, he told himself. *One life, to save hundreds.*

'God watch my aim,' he whispered, just before he loosed the arrow.

The shaft flew from the bow, skimming over the crowd towards its target. The sergeant turned to his comrade, his mouth open as he shouted a command. The arrowhead punched through his cheek and the force dislocated his jaw. Teeth shattered and blood fountained from his mouth. His head snapped back and his shield and spear fell from his dead hands. The guards around him froze in shock.

For the briefest of moments, everything became still and quiet, the only sound that of Friar Tuck spurring on Fury as he charged alongside the stream of people, towards the gate, one meaty hand clutching the reins, the other holding his oak staff at the ready. Then the pandemonium rose again, the panicking civilians seizing the advantage to rip spears from the hands of sergeants and use them to clear a path to the gate.

The sound of it wrenching open and the cheer of the men and women as they began funnelling through it gave Robin a burst of energy as he and the remainder of his group charged forward. They barged their way along with the crowd, hopping over sergeants laying prostrate on the ground, dead already from the crush. They had made it. They were out.

The citizens of Nottingham spread like spraying water, hurdling the low stonewalls lining either side of the dirt path, streaking across the hilly fields that stretched away from Nottingham. Robin tore off his hat and raised his longbow as he stood at the side of the road.

'Listen to me!' he cried. 'Everyone make for

Sherwood! Make for Robin Hood's camp! Follow the Friar!'

'Follow me!' Friar Tuck yelled, throwing off his hat as he dug his heels into Fury's flanks, the horse galloping north towards the forest. All who heard Robin's command ran in the Friar's wake; soon, some of those who hadn't heard noticed where their compatriots were running, and began following as fast as they could.

Robin ran back towards the gate, telling everyone who scrambled past him to follow Tuck.

Stooping low to avoid the bolts shot from the sergeants on the walls, he heard dull thuds as people were struck. He knew that not everyone was going to make it out.

He flattened himself against the gatehouse, next to Marian. Beside her, Little John, Much and the Butcher were urging the people forward, bending to pick up those who lost their balance in the chaos, dragging people before they were trampled into the dirt.

A hundred or so may have escaped so far, but there was ten times that number converging on the gate – which was only wide enough for eight people to run through at once.

'Make for Sherwood!' Robin kept repeating.

The harsh cry of the Sheriff's bugle, its call repeated over and over again, increased the desperation of the crowd. He heard the breaking of bones and the cries of shock and pain as the crush got more desperate. He heard the neighing of horses and the trampling of hooves. He saw the mounted sergeants swinging clubs and swords. He saw some people turn and run back into Nottingham for their own safety.

And then he saw them stop and turn back.

He felt Marian clutching at him, pulling him away from the gate.

'We cannot hope to get them all out, Robin,' she said.

'But why are they—' Robin's question was answered before he had finished it. Straining on tiptoes, he could just about see the two streets that led into the main square. Scores of the Undead charged, running with that same chaotic stride Robin had seen before. Spit and blood flew from their mouths, baring broken and yellowed teeth. They fell upon the civilians in packs. Robin knew from the cut-off screams that the fallen were being devoured. He saw small children sprint away from the gate, only to be tackled to the ground. He saw gnarled, clawed hands reaching into the mass of the terrified living. He heard the pleas for mercy, the prayers for rescue.

Marian was right. It was hopeless. His limbs were numb now, offering no resistance as Marian and the Butcher dragged him away from the town gate.

What seemed like three dozen armoured enforcers of the Sheriff on horseback trampled their way towards the gate. As he watched in mounting horror, Robin realised that none of the Sheriff's men showed any fear of what was happening, no fear of the Undead fiends feasting on the flesh of fleeing people.

And they had not done so at any point.

Why?

The sound of the gate slamming closed seemed to rattle the air. Outside, some of the people turned back and hammered on the wooden beams, calling out the names of their loved ones. Robin knew that the Undead had torn apart families as brutally as they had ripped the flesh off their victims' bones.

From behind the closed gate, the fearful cries of those caught by the Plague Undead, and the screams and shrieks of agony as they were bitten or scratched told a grim tale of what was happening.

'Come on, Robin,' said Marian, as she and the Butcher pulled him away to where Little John and Much were already running in the direction of the ragged stream of people making for Sherwood.

But Robin's legs would not move. His eyes were fixed on the Nottingham gate, his head full of confusion and his heart weighed down with regret.

In one day, Robin had led his mentor to his death, and failed the people of Nottingham – the people he had always sworn to protect.

The people he had let down.

Part Two

Chapter Eleven

Dawn rose on the Outlaws' camp, though no one had slept since they reached it some time the night before. The dark hours had been filled with bitter tears, unanswerable questions and useless prayers. The first light hour was no different.

Barely a blade of grass in the glade was visible for the people. All of the tents had been flattened, some of the cloth used as blankets for people laying out in the open. Strangers huddled together for warmth and comfort.

There were nearly two hundred in the camp, with the addition of those who escaped Nottingham. It was the largest group Robin had ever gathered to him at one time – only this was not a fighting force, but a band of frightened, confused people on the verge of falling apart.

'And they're looking to me for help,' Robin told Marian as they walked through the trees a short way from the camp. They weren't walking anywhere in particular – Robin just wanted to get away from the fear and anxiety.

'You couldn't have foreseen this,' said Marian. 'No one could have.'

'Why would the Sheriff order his men to close the gates?' Robin asked, voicing the thought that had recurred to him most frequently during the night. 'Why were the sergeants not afraid of the Undead?'

Looking across, Robin could see Marian's tongue prodding her cheek, as it always did when she was concentrating. It was an expression that Robin usually found amusing – but at that moment, he felt like he would find nothing amusing for the rest of his life.

'I just don't know,' she said finally.

Robin leaned on a birch tree and felt like he could punch through the trunk. 'Will always told me to think things through,' Robin said. 'Think of everything, and ask every question that comes to mind. So let's do that. The sergeants weren't afraid, or even shocked, which means they knew about the Undead. Not only that – they knew they were safe. They showed no fear of being attacked, nor of getting the plague themselves.'

'They were heavily armoured,' said Marian. 'Even more than usual.'

'Yes,' said Robin. 'And they closed the gates before the Curfew Bell. Why? Because they didn't want anyone to leave.'

'But could the Sheriff really *want* to do that?' Marian asked. 'As bad as he is, is he capable of condemning the whole town in that way? And for God's sake, why?'

'I don't know why,' said Robin.

Marian rubbed her tired, puffy eyes. 'None of that matters right now – what *does* matter is that we have a lot of frightened people to look after.'

Robin's gaze dropped to the ground, where Marian's shadow fell over his feet. 'I don't know if I can,' he told her. 'There's so many people there. And if Will was still here, then maybe I...' He laced his fingers behind his head and looked at the treetops. 'I failed him,' he continued. 'I told him he was too old to ride with us, then let him talk me into changing my mind. If it wasn't for me...'

'Look at me, Robin.' Marian's voice was gentle.

But he could not look at her. He could barely look at her shadow. Marian's palm caught Robin flush across his left cheek, and he looked at her, startled.

'You can cry about Will later,' she said. 'Right now, there are people in that camp that need you. Surrender to your self-pity, and you really *will* have failed them.'

Marian walked back to the camp.

Robin followed her. He had no more hope than he did before, but he did have a little more determination. She was right – a leader should not fall apart. A leader had to be strong for those who looked up to him. He paused when he heard noises away to his right.

Footsteps.

Two slow and too even to be the footsteps of the Undead – but that did not stop Robin drawing Will's sword from his hip as he flattened himself against a tree. Marian stopped and turned, eyeing him curiously. Robin placed a finger to his lips. She pointed a finger at herself, then made a circular gesture: *I'll loop round the back of the intruder.*

Robin nodded, and placed his finger against his lips again: *Be careful and quiet.* He tapped his ear once: *Be alert.*

Marian slipped away, as silently as possible, and Robin closed his eyes as he tried to focus on the sounds. They were off to his right, maybe fifty feet away, and slowly getting closer. It couldn't have been one of his Outlaws – these footsteps clearly belonged to someone who was creeping, sneaking around. Someone who didn't want to be heard.

Robin held Will's sword tighter, the blade angled down and the grip unfamiliar in his hand. He took deep breaths through his nose to calm his nerves and realised that, even though he was in Sherwood Forest – his domain – he was on edge.

He was scared.

When the footsteps came within ten feet of him, Robin braced himself. When they were within five feet, he burst from his hiding place and drove his sword forward, holding the edge of the blade against the throat of a pale young man, who froze and held up his hands in a gesture of surrender. Robin saw that he wore leather gauntlets. A red-and-black cloak flowed behind him.

'A sergeant,' said Robin, anger replacing his nerves. 'Come to spy on us, have you?'

The sergeant shook his head, keeping his hands raised. 'I swear to you, good Robin,' he said, 'I mean you no harm.'

'I don't believe you,' said Robin, as Marian came up from the rear. She patted at the sergeant's back, giving him a start, and then felt around his waist, knees and ankles.

'He's not carrying any weapons,' she said.

Robin lowered his blade, though his eyes remained

fixed on the sergeant. His face looked drawn and haunted. He breathed heavily, through exertion or fear – perhaps both.

'You're taking a risk,' said Robin, 'walking in this forest, wearing that uniform.'

The sergeant cast a brief look at himself. 'I was going to throw it off,' he said. 'But the night was cold, and I had nothing else.'

Robin stared at the sergeant for a long moment. 'What are you doing here?'

'What happened in Nottingham was...' The sergeant shook his head, the words not coming to him. 'I escaped through the gate,' he said, 'when you challenged us. I saw those terrifying fiends and my fear got the better of me, I'm ashamed to say. I... I didn't know where else to go.'

'How do we know you're telling the truth?' asked Marian.

'You don't,' said the sergeant. 'But I'm happy to convince you.'

'And how do you plan to do that?' asked Robin.

'I know some things that you don't,' said the sergeant, lowering his hands slowly.

They made a ragged triangle, Robin and Marian

facing the sergeant. 'We've been under orders,' he said, 'all of us. The Sheriff warned that people would be falling very ill, and that it was our job to make sure that no one in Nottingham panicked.'

Marian nodded. 'You hid the sick people in the Sheriff's castle.'

'Yes, my lady,' said the sergeant.

'And what happened to them when they were there?' asked Robin.

'We put them in the dungeons,' the sergeant replied. 'We thought we were leaving them to die.'

Robin felt his jaw tighten as he remembered the fate of Little John's family. 'But they didn't die, did they?'

'We had no idea that they would become...whatever they are now,' said the sergeant. 'We were just doing what we were told.'

'And the Sheriff didn't tell you why he was giving you these orders?' asked Robin.

The sergeant shook his head again.

'There's one thing I don't understand,' said Marian. 'How did the Sheriff know the plague had hit the city?'

'We think,' said the sergeant, 'that it's to do with the Witch.'

Robin looked to Marian, and saw her face showed the anxiety he felt gripping his chest. He looked back at the sergeant. 'A short woman?' he said. 'Very pale, with a pointed chin?'

'Yes, that's her,' said the sergeant.

Marian gasped. 'Mother Maudlin...'

Robin ran his hand over his face, growling in frustration. 'I should have suspected,' he said. 'Of course it was her – some sort of black magic...'

The sergeant looked almost afraid to ask his next question. 'Who is she, then?'

Robin relaxed his hands and looked up at the forest canopy. Through the gaps, he could see a dull, grey sky. It was as if the sun had turned away from the world. Robin could hardly blame it if it had.

'Evil,' he said, looking at the sergeant. 'Mother Maudlin is pure evil.'

Chapter Twelve

While Robin Hood was struggling to keep his camp from falling apart, the Sheriff of Nottingham stood at the top the north turret of his castle and looked out over the town that he once controlled – the town that was now no more than an open tomb where the Undead roamed.

After closing the town gates, the Sheriff had recalled every one of his sergeants to the castle, which was the only safe place in the region now. Some civilians tried to break down the doors, but they were too well fortified. The Undead grew in number, rampaging through the streets, scratching and biting everyone in their path.

Now, as dawn rose, the agonised cries of the dying, and the menacing groans of the reawakened Undead filled the air. The streets were awash with the black sludge that they expelled, clogging the central gutters, its stench choking the air for miles.

Every civilian left behind had been infected. And soon, all of them would be transformed. The Sheriff estimated that it was around eight hundred and fifty people in all. A little short of the thousand he had promised Prince John – because he had not bargained for that damned Outlaw showing up.

The Outlaw had cost the Sheriff about a hundred and fifty people. But surely over eight hundred was sufficient for the Prince's plans? The Sheriff hoped it was. The Prince was due to arrive that morning, and even a man as fearsome as the Sheriff dreaded how he might react to disappointment.

The Sheriff slammed his fist on the battlement, barely feeling the impact. Robin Hood! Always there to get in the way. Always getting one over on him, always spoiling *something*. As he turned his gaze away from the tomb-town, the Sheriff wondered if even the land, power and wealth promised to him by Prince John would be enough to satisfy him.

Could he ever be content while Robin Hood still breathed? What use was money and influence if he would always be remembered as the man who could not defeat a common criminal?

Prince John arrived within half an hour, having made the journey from Worcester.

The Sheriff had hosted royalty before, but he had never greeted so strange an entourage as that which the Prince, de facto ruler of England in the prolonged absence of his older brother,brought to his castle that morning.

The procession crossing the castle grounds was led by two knights in gleaming silver armour, with the Prince behind them, flanked by two more knights. About thirty soldiers marched at the rear. But there were no packhorses or hunting dogs. There was no outrider bearing livery, no sound of the clarion call to signal their approach. And there was just a single wagon loaded with the barest essentials – blankets, extra cloaks, food – when the Sheriff would normally have expected a dozen carts or more, bearing cooking utensils, luxury clothes and garments, jewels and treasures.

Prince John was travelling as light as a royal man dared. And yet, as the Sheriff met him in the Great Hall, he could see that the Prince was not vulnerable.

Not in the least. His taut features – described as 'rat-like' by those who preferred their heads separated from their shoulders – were unmoving. His grey eyes shone with confidence and determination. He was focused. His tall, wiry frame glided through the Great Hall, his black and sky blue cape fluttering and billowing behind him. He looked like he was already the King, and was just missing a crown. His footsteps were muffled by the clattering and grinding of the armour worn by the brace of knights who followed him everywhere.

'My Lord,' said the Sheriff, kneeling before the Prince. 'As promised, I have surrendered my town of Nottingham to you for your...army.'

The Sheriff felt the Prince's hands on his shoulders, and took that as his cue to rise and stand face-to-face with the man who might well be the next King of England.

'I am grateful to you, Sheriff,' said the Prince. 'I know agreeing to my demands could not have been easy.'

'I did it gladly, my lord,' said the Sheriff.

The Prince's lips curled in a sneer. 'Gladly?' he echoed. 'I did not want you to *like* what you have done, Sheriff. What we have done is unholy, despicable... But, sadly, it is necessary.'

The Sheriff bowed in apology, feeling his cheeks flush with anger.

The Prince strolled to a window in the west wall, his knights stalking him like silver shadows. He looked out over the tomb-town of Nottingham. When he turned back, the Sheriff could see that his face wore an expression of excited disbelief – as though even he was shocked at what they had done.

'Remarkable,' he breathed. 'Absolutely remarkable.' Then he lightly shook his head, as if chasing away his own thoughts. 'Soon, Mother Maudlin will march my new army on London. And we will claim the capital.'

The Sheriff marched over to the Prince, regretting it almost instantly – to stand by the window was to be kissed by the air of death from outside, although it did not seem to affect the Prince.

'That's if the Outlaw, Robin Hood, doesn't stand in your way.' Mother Maudlin had appeared behind them, giving even Prince John a start. The knights began to draw their swords, but the Prince raised his hand.

'At ease,' he said. 'She's a…friend.' He looked at the Witch. 'What do you mean, Mother?'

Mother Maudlin's face was a picture of innocence. 'Oh… Has the Sheriff not told you?'

The Prince looked from the Sheriff to Mother Mauldin and back again. 'Told me what?'

The Witch flounced away, her black robes and white hair trailing behind her. A slender hand went to her forehead, pressing the pentagram etching. 'Oh dear, I've spoken out of turn! I'm always doing that.'

The Sheriff averted his gaze from the Prince – the gall of the Witch, to betray him when he had done so much and worked so hard to give them their hideous army!

'What is she talking about, Sheriff?' the Prince asked.

'The Outlaw they call Robin Hood,' the Sheriff began, 'was in Nottingham yesterday. He caused a riot, and tried to evacuate the town.'

The Prince's face paled as he took angry breaths through his nose, bull-like. 'And he was not caught or killed? Why not?'

'He escaped,' the Sheriff told him. 'Along with a few civilians.'

'More than a few, Sheriff,' laughed Maudlin.

'How many?' asked the Prince.

The Sheriff sighed. 'My sergeants estimated around a hundred, my liege.'

The Prince marched up to the Sheriff. His knights followed, hands on their swords. 'So over a hundred people left Nottingham yesterday?'

The Sheriff nodded. 'I'm afraid so. But what harm can they do?'

'What harm, you ask?' the Prince bellowed. 'What happens when they reach the nearest town and spread word of the Plague? What happens when that word reaches London? What happens when alert eyes along the roads see our army heading South?

'I'll tell you what happens then, you useless glorified clerk! We lose the element of surprise! The people of London will be ready for us. They will fight back.'

The Sheriff felt his face tighten in a grimace. He had gone from jubilant to bereft in mere moments. And all because that Witch had to open her rotton mouth.

No, it wasn't the Witch's fault. Not really. It was Robin Hood, thwarting him again – even without being anywhere near the castle. That Outlaw always managed to somehow get in his way!

'What use are you now?' said the Prince, flapping a dismissive hand at the Sheriff as he turned away from him. 'Men, throw him in his own dungeon – I will chop off his head when I have the time to spare!'

The Prince's knights grabbed the Sheriff's arms. He struggled, but these were well-trained men. He was helpless to stop himself being dragged across the Great Hall, no matter how much he thrashed and kicked. In desperation, an idea came to him. He knew something about the Prince – a weak spot that might complement the Sheriff's hatred for Robin Hood.

'My lord,' he shouted, when he was almost at the

doorway. 'I can still help you. I can silence Robin Hood – and his Outlaw Queen!'

'Halt!' cried the Prince. The knights stopped dragging the Sheriff, though they maintained a tight grip on him as the Prince strode the length of the Great Hall.

'What do you speak of, Sheriff?' the Prince asked. 'Do you mean to tell me that the Lady Marian has reunited with that criminal?'

The Sheriff nodded. 'My sergeants assure me,' he said, 'that she was at the gate yesterday, helping Robin Hood get civilians out of Nottingham.'

Prince John pondered, pinching his bottom lip. 'Well, this does change things...'

The Prince's face cleared and he looked at his knights. 'Let him go...*for now*.'

The knights released the Sheriff with a shove that almost sent him rolling along the floor of the Great Hall.

The Prince stared at him with cold, unblinking eyes. 'You, Sheriff, and a company of your men will join Mother Maudlin and her Undead charges in Sherwood Forest. The Undead will kill the Outlaws, and any civilians who followed them, while you capture the woman who is, by rights, mine. It seems only right that she is by my side as my queen when I am crowned. But, Sheriff...if you fail me again, there will be a far worse fate in store for you than the dungeon. Is that understood?'

The Sheriff dropped to his knees, trying to keep the grin off his face. Lady Marian was Prince John's weak spot and he clearly could not resist the temptation to finally claim her.

'I understand, my lord,' said the Sheriff.

Without another word, the Prince swept from the Great Hall, taking his knights with him and leaving the Sheriff alone with the Witch.

When he was confident that the Prince was out of earshot, the Sheriff rounded on Mother Maudlin. 'Your meddling almost cost me my head,' he told her.

The Witch shrugged. 'I'm on no one's side. You were lucky, though – you think fast on your feet when you're being dragged off them.' Her laughter cannoned off the walls, ming to stab right through the Sheriff's head and making him cringe.

'Yes, I was lucky,' he said. 'But I might not be so again. I should get to work, and hope I can find the Outlaws' camp.'

He began to head out of the Great Hall, when the Witch's voice called him back. 'I can help you,' she said.

The Sheriff stopped in the doorway and turned around. Mercifully, Mother Maudlin had stayed where she was, rather than chase him like a fluttering spirit. 'How can you help?' he asked. 'Can you...*see* the camp?'

Mother Maudlin just smiled, and walked to the window. Sliding the sleeve of her robe up one sore-spotted arm, she thrust it through the window and issued that same hideous, snake-like call he had heard her emit in his dungeon. After a moment, she drew her arm back from the window, and beckoned the Sheriff over.

The Sheriff joined her and looked out. When he saw who – or, rather, what – was out there, he smiled.

Approaching the castle was the Undead form of another of the Sheriff's enemies.

Will Scarlet.

'We don't know the location of the Outlaws' camp,' said Mother Maudlin. 'But we know a man who did.'

Chapter Thirteen

'Do you believe him?'

Much was perched on a low branch of the Major Oak. Beside him, Little John leaned against the trunk. Robin, Marian, Friar Tuck and the Butcher stood facing them. Their backs were to the glade, and to the people in it, but Robin did not have to look to know that all eyes were on them. They spoke in low voices, because Robin did not want everyone to know who was involved – who the sergeant in the forest had said was responsible for the Plague that had torn their town to pieces.

'I do,' said Robin. 'To get this close to our camp, dressed in his uniform, with people as angry and desperate as those we have here, was a great risk.'

The Butcher nodded. 'If someone else had found him,' he said, 'they would probably have killed him before he opened his mouth.'

'It would have been the right thing,' said Little John. His voice was low, and his shoulders were slumped as if a great weight was on them. A weight even Little John struggled to bear.

'Where is he now?' asked Friar Tuck. 'The sergeant?'

'In the camp,' said Marian. 'We had him dump his cloak, of course. For his own safety.'

Little John shook his head. 'Hiding among the victims, eh? If I find him—'

'We know more than we did before,' said Robin, changing the subject. 'We have an idea what we're up against now.'

'Mother Maudlin,' said Tuck, crossing himself and mumbling a prayer. 'That woman is the Devil's daughter.'

Much hopped down off the branch. 'Is it really her?' he asked. 'I never thought she was real. My father used to speak of her, but I thought he was just trying to scare me.'

Robin nodded at Much. 'She is real,' he said. 'A real witch. She practices a dark form of magic, but I never thought even she'd be capable of conjuring something like this.'

'And she and the Sheriff are working together?' Marian asked.

'If I know Mother Maudlin,' said Robin, 'the Sheriff is working *for* her.'

'Have you seen the Witch before?' Much asked.

'No,' said Robin.

'Then, how do you know she's real?' the Butcher asked.

His hand drifted unconsciously to Will Scarlet's sword, as memories fluttered through his mind. 'Five years ago, Will and I sought her out. We heard that she dwelt in Paplewick, in a well-hidden shack.' Robin looked down at the sword at his hip. 'We intended to kill her. We searched for three days, but never found a trace of her or her dwelling.'

Much frowned. 'Why had you gone looking for a Witch?'

The older Outlaws glanced at each other.

'What is it?' Much asked. 'Why are you looking at each other like that?'

'Because,' Robin replied gently, 'it was the witch who informed on your father to the Sheriff.'

Much's mouth opened and closed as he looked from one Outlaw to the next. 'You mean...she...' His face crumpled. Beside him, Little John clasped a meaty hand around his neck.

Robin wanted to say something, but no words came to mind. No one said anything for several minutes, while Much cried, comforted by Little John and Marian.

'I hope she finds us,' Much said, his voice strained.

'So I can kill her.'

Robin said nothing. He turned away and tried not to catch one of the two hundred pairs of anxious-looking eyes staring right at him.

He knew that the worst was far from over.

The day passed. No one spoke much. The camp was deathly quiet.

Robin arranged with the Butcher to organise groups of men to go hunting the next morning. He asked Little John to help with this, to keep his mind occupied.

Friar Tuck heard many confessions throughout the day; scores and scores of people queued up to speak to him, and hear his prayers.

It was with relief that Robin noticed a calm resilience settle over the camp by late afternoon, as the sky began to slowly darken. Sherwood Forest at night was eerie at the best of times.

'Robin?'

Tuck's voice startled Robin out of his reverie. He was sat between two thick roots of the Major Oak, watching the silent, sombre camp. Tuck stood over him, a soft smile on his face.

'Yes, Friar?' said Robin.

'Would you like me to take your confession?' Tuck asked.

Robin shook his head.

Tuck sat beside him with a grunt. 'There's something I'd like to discuss with you,' he said.

'Please,' said Robin.

'I don't think we should stay here too long,' Tuck said. 'There is no telling what will happen next. We should get as far away from Nottingham as possible.'

Robin looked over the camp. 'There are close to two hundred in my care,' he said. 'It will be hard to keep them ordered and safe if we leave the camp.'

'I know,' said the Friar. 'But we have to try. Staying here is dangerous.'

'Where would we go?'

'To Fountain's Abbey.'

'Lincoln?' said Robin, thinking it over. 'That's several days' walk. Several days where we would be exposed. Vulnerable.'

'We're vulnerable here,' said Tuck, waving his arm over the glade. 'And I fear that simply staying in one place will feel to these people like waiting for death. If we take to the road, they will have purpose, a destination – something to stay alive for.'

'We don't know the way to Lincoln,' Robin said.

'I do,' said Tuck. 'I studied there. I know the Abbot. He will give us sanctuary, and guide us through these...dark days. The dead walk, Robin. And you know what that foretells.'

'The Day of Judgement,' Robin said. 'The end of all things.'

Tuck nodded. 'The journey to Fountains' Abbey might give these poor souls heart and courage.'

'Let me think on it,' sighed Robin. 'We'll decide in the morning.'

Friar Tuck patted Robin's shoulder and stood up. 'I'll see if anyone needs me,' he said.

Robin rested his head against the trunk of the Major Oak, his mind full of thoughts and plans all tumbling over one another. His head was starting to hurt from it. He shook himself, rubbed his face with his hands to stave off his tiredness, and decided to see to his men.

He stood up, and found himself face to face with Will Scarlet.

Chapter Fourteen

Will Scarlet rounded the Major Oak and advanced on Robin with hands shaped like the talons of an eagle swooping on its prey. His nails were jagged, cruel and the same shade of brownish yellow as his teeth, which were bared in a hungry snarl as blood-flecked drool gushed from his mouth and stained his white beard. His left eye streamed thick, bubbling blood, and his pale-grey right eye pierced through the gloom.

'Stay back!' Robin called, stumbling into the clearing as he drew his sword – Will's sword. Behind him, he heard his most trusted Outlaws, running hither and thither, scooping up weapons as they came to join him. Further behind, the civilians and other Outlaws lost all composure. Robin heard shouts of 'Demon!' But the people weren't running away. They were frozen in fear.

'Cross formation!' yelled Marian. The Outlaws surrounded the rotting, walking carcass of Will Scarlet at four points. Friar Tuck, staff at the ready, flanked the Undead Will on the left, with Robin on the right and Little John and Lady Marian in front and behind.

'How did Will find his way back?' Much squeaked, hovering behind Robin. Robin could hear some of them shouting 'Kill it!' He could hear others running for their lives into the forest.

'Robin, sir,' said the Butcher, his voice creaking like a rotten branch as he stood at Little John's side, his spear poised. 'Do we…?'

Robin felt the eyes of his men on him. Only he could make this decision. This was the great 'privilege' of leadership.

With a blood-wet growl, the Undead Outlaw lurched forwards, taking Robin by surprise and knocking the sword out of his hands. Robin landed on his back, looking up into the partially eroded face of his mentor. Robin could only reach out and clutch at the fiend's wrists as it fell upon him.

He felt skin that was damp from the decay of an unfinished death, the muscle beneath yielding under his fingertips. Soft flesh and cold blood trickled down Robin's hands like drained water. As he struggled to keep the claws away from his face, Robin felt his fingers close around bone.

Robin heard Friar Tuck's desperate warning, 'Watch for his nails! He must not break your skin!'

The fiend was impervious to Much's kicks, and

Friar Tuck's jabs with his staff. It was too strong to be pulled off by the Butcher, and did not seem to feel Lady Marian's arrows thudding into its ribs. Its empty eyes were fixed on Robin, tears of blood tumbling from them and dripping onto Robin's cheeks, mingling with the fetid drool that dangled from the fiend's lips and beard.

The stench of death filled Robin's nose, making his throat close with vomit and his eyes burn with tears. Blindly, Robin continued to struggle, using all his might to turn the Fiend's wrists so that his cruel nails faced away from him.

'Stand aside!' Out of the corner of his eye, Robin saw Little John pick up Will Scarlet's sword. Then came the hoarse battle-cry that Robin had heard so many times before, followed by the *swish* of a sword as it sliced the air and slid through the flesh of the Undead Outlaw.

Robin felt the weight on top of him lurch to his right and he let the fiend fall away. He released his grip on its rotting wrists and rolled to his left. He wiped his hands on his cloak, staining his Lincoln Green with rancid blood and sludgy flesh that was once his friend's. He hacked and spat to clear his mouth of the taste of Will's corpse.

Robin waved Little John's helping hand away. He looked back to the Undead Will, who thrashed and floundered on the floor. Its wrists bore dents the size and shape of Robin's fingers.

Its neck had been skewered by the sword.

'And still it lives!' muttered Friar Tuck, crossing himself.

Robin knew what he had to do. 'Much,' he said. 'My bow.'

The Miller's Son handed Robin his bow and quiver. He nocked an arrow to his bow. The creaking of the string was unbearably loud in Robin's ears as he took aim at the thrashing *thing* that wore Will's body.

But his hand was quivering in a way that it never had before. He did not trust his aim. And with the Undead Will's erratic motions, his target was small and awkward.

But I cannot miss this shot, Robin told himself. *Our friend may still live, buried somewhere beneath those layers of evil. I must not add to his eternal suffering. I must aim true.*

Robin drew his bowstring back as far as it would go, keeping his eyes on the fiend's chest, and not the face that so resembled Robin's lost friend.

'I am sorry.'

Robin put an arrow into the heart that had once been Will Scarlet's. It pierced the flesh and the fiend fell, hitting the grass with a dull thud. Robin wiped his eyes with his sleeve and started to turn away, when the sound came again.

Slick. Blood-wet. Rasping.

The Undead Will still endured.

Robin turned to Tuck. 'Go to the people. Tell them...' He thought for a long moment. Then he nodded to himself. 'Tell them we will organise ourselves and make for Fountains' Abbey.'

Robin Hood was left alone by the Major Oak – alone with the moving dead body of his mentor. He had failed Will once – it was his responsibility not to fail him again.

Slowly, Robin turned to face the Undead Will for what he vowed would be the last time. The fiend sat straight up. Dark blood left its body through the hole that Robin had left in its heart.

It trickles, Robin realised, *when it should gush*. That was why the fiend had not been killed. How could an arrow through the heart kill it, when its heart had long stopped beating?

Robin reached behind him for another arrow – an action that was as instinctive for Robin Hood as breathing was for any normal man, now seemed strange and foreign.

The Undead Will crawled towards him.

The hum of the bowstring seemed to be the only sound in the forest. Robin's arrow slammed into Will's skull, pinning it to the grass.

'Mother?'

The Sheriff did not care much for the witch, but even he was alarmed when she fell to her knees. They were somewhere in Sherwood Forest, deeper than he had ever been before. Mother Maudlin was following the scent left by the Undead Will Scarlet, who was hopefully leading them to Robin Hood's camp.

Knowing he was so close to finally raiding the Outlaws' secret home gave the Sheriff tingles. He could barely keep the smile off his face.

The Sheriff, whose horse was at the head of a squad of his sergeants, rode forward and drew to a stop by the Witch. She was shaking her head, her face twisted with grief.

'Oh... Oh...' The Witch's pointed chin looked dagger sharp as she bared her teeth in a raging snarl. Her breaths came in rumbling, ragged snorts and gasps, like those of the Undead.

'What is it?' the Sheriff asked.

'That cursed Outlaw,' she spat. 'He killed one of my babies.'

'They can be killed?' he asked incredulously. 'I thought they were invincible?'

'The Outlaw got lucky,' said the Witch, getting to her feet, her cheeks glistening with tears.

Mother Maudlin looked ahead, into the forest gloom. The Sheriff knew that a small army of Undead were being steered by Maudlin, guiding them like a ship through still waters. And there were others too, the Sheriff knew – more and more Undead waiting in the forest, awaiting the Witch's command.

'We are so close now,' she said.

The Sheriff saw her turn her hands palm-up – that familiar posture of control and intent.

'I will send my babies in now,' she said. 'Then we can attack from the other side.'

'Sounds good,' said the Sheriff. 'But remember – they must not touch the woman.'

The Witch said nothing. She just curled her lips back over her teeth and sent her hissing call into the darkness of the forest.

In Sherwood's secret glade, Robin stood over Will's

corpse for a long moment. Only when he was certain the body would not rise again, did he turn and join his friends in the camp.

They were gathering people to them in groups. As he got closer, Robin could see relief on many of the faces, but panic and worry on others. He saw Marian and the Butcher look on helplessly as a few terrified civilians broke away and bolted for the trees.

Robin reached the middle of the clearing and was about to call after those who had fled, but there was no need – they were turning around and running back into the camp.

Chapter Fifteen

'Undead!' went the call. 'The Undead are coming!'

Everyone gathered together in the middle of the camp. Robin shouted to be heard above the petrified cries: 'Outlaws! Arm up and make a ring around the civilians. All weapons must face outwards. Do not break the formation.'

Robin's sixty Outlaws formed a circle around the townsfolk, who argued among themselves as they turned this way and that. They wanted to run, but there was no escape now.

'We should flee!'

'But there will be more Undead out there!'

'We're trapped here like pigs in a pen!'

Robin wanted to reassure them somehow, but what would be the point of trying? They were out in the open, it was growing dark – and they were under attack from the Plague Undead. And of their two hundred, only sixty had weapons.

'Archers!' Robin cried. 'Space yourselves out along the circle. Keep the Undead at a distance. We must not let them get close, do you understand me?'

He could hear the Undead now, hear their ragged running steps beyond the shadows of the trees.

They would soon be in the glade.

Little John turned to the nearest archer, a skinny minstrel called Alan A'Dale. 'Gimme that!' said John. 'Your aim is worse than your singing. You take this in case the line is broken.' He shoved his double-headed axe at the boy, who nearly capsized with the weight of it.

Robin felt a flutter of optimism – Little John was a deadly archer. They would have a better chance of survival with him shooting out of the circle. Robin held his bow ready, aiming between the trees on the southern edge of the glade, waiting for their enemy to emerge.

He heard them before he saw them. The blood-wet snarls of flesh-hungry fiends, the breaking of branches and flattening of foliage as they trampled towards them.

Then the chaotic company of corpses crashed through the trees and burst into the Outlaws' camp. Five at first – running in a ragged line, arms wheeling as though they were running downhill and off-balance.

'Aim for the head!' Robin yelled, as he, Marian,

Little John and two more archers facing south let fly. The first line of fiends fell face-first on to the grass, barely taking three steps into the glade. But in the time it took the Outlaws to ready their second volley, the next ragged line had breached the glade, making it nearly twenty feet across.

They might have been dead men running, but they were *so fast*.

'Keep shooting!'

The forest was filled with the thrum of bowstrings, the *whoosh* of arrows, the *squelch* of broken flesh and pierced brains.

And finally the thud of bodies hitting the ground, dead at last.

But as the second line fell, the third had covered half the distance towards the Outlaws. Robin barely had time to set his aim before he shot his third arrow.

'Back!' he cried. 'Move back – maintain the distance!'

The writhing ball of horrified people shuffled along closer to the north edge of the glade, although there was no way to move a group that size fast enough to match the speed of the Undead.

To Robin's right, Marian was loosing arrows with speed and accuracy. To his left, Little John was almost snapping the Minstrel's bowstring with every shot.

But with each line of Undead that fell, those running in their wake were getting closer and closer, even with the Outlaws and civilian survivors shuffling back as fast as they could. Robin realised with sickening dread that soon the battle would have to be fought at close quarters.

There was no way that everyone in the glade would survive.

'Now gimme this back!' Little John growled as he snatched his axe from Alan A'Dale, just as two fiends launched themselves at him. With a yell, Little John took a step forward and swung, taking the first Undead's head clean off with one blade, and splitting a second one's skull down the middle with the other.

'Keep fighting!' Robin cried, as he slung his bow over his shoulder and drew Will Scarlet's sword. 'Stab them in the head, chop them off! Aim for the brain!'

Robin stepped up next to Little John, swinging Will's blade with all his strength. Undead fell either side of them, little more than brownish-yellow blurs carrying a sickening stench. As he struck them, Robin noticed the ragged, blood-spattered clothes they wore, identifying those of a yeomen, a serf, and a peasant woman.

But he could not think of them as who they once were. They were not people now. They were fiends who needed to die.

'Keep moving back!' he shouted, seeing Friar Tuck step up alongside him. The holy man had snapped off one end of his staff so that he could stab the jagged end into Undead skulls.

'In the name of the Lord,' cried the Friar as his makeshift spear went through the forehead of a fiend dressed in the black gown of a working woman, 'I send you to Hell!'

The circle was moving back, the Butcher and Much doing a good job of cajoling the frightened people to the north edge of the glade. Robin had expected some of them to break from the group and try running for it, but no one did – he assumed that Sherwood Forest at night, with an autumn mist descending and the Plague Undead lurking, was just too frightening a prospect.

But the Undead did not stop coming. The Outlaws had formed a wavy line facing south, swinging swords, clubs, staffs and axes. Robin's hair was already slick with sweat, and his arms began burning with tiredness, threatening to throw off his aim. As scalps went flying, trailing chunks of mushy brains and drops of blackened blood, he knew they could not keep this up for much longer.

They had to get away. But how was he going to do that in a flat clearing surrounded by trees?

The Undead were coming from the south, so Robin and his followers would have to head north. They would have almost no visibility in the woods, but they might find hiding places. Maybe they could use the trees to their advantage, picking off the Undead as they trampled across the uneven forest ground.

Robin placed himself back to back with Marian, whose sword was arcing gracefully, cutting down fiends with ease. 'You must lead them north,' he said. 'John, the Friar and I will hold the line here for as long as we can – you get the people to safety.'

'I'm not going anywhere,' said Marian, as she hacked her sword diagonally, taking off not only a fiend's head, but its left shoulder and arm too.

'You must,' said Robin, swinging his sword upwards from the ground at a fiend in the form of a fat man with greasy black hair, the blade striking him first under the jaw and then splitting the rest of his head like a banana skin. 'Find the road to Lincoln, make for Fountains' Abbey.'

'We'll kill more Undead if I'm here,' said Marian,

whirling her sword before slicing it right to left, taking off another head at eye level. With a strange kind of exhilarated disgust, Robin stamped on the half-eyeballs that had landed at his feet before slamming the point of his sword through the nose of an Undead tanner, ripping it free and having to shield his face from the rain of blood and bone fragments.

That one got very close, he thought. *Too close*.

'But we'll save more if you lead them out,' Robin said.

'Will you follow us?' Marian asked, slipping behind Robin while he chopped and stabbed at fiend after fiend.

'Yes,' Robin replied. 'We will follow you. Go, now!'

Robin felt Marian's hand on his shoulder for the briefest of moments, then she was gone. He heard her command the townspeople to follow her. He hoped he could keep his promise to her.

Beside him, Little John's grunts of exertion took on a tone of violent delight. Each of his strikes was delivered with a triumphant, 'Ha!'

'Must be the whole town of Nottingham come to kill us, Robin!' he said.

'Looks that way, my friend,' said Robin, daring to step up through the rushing line of fiends and attacking three in quick succession. He almost tripped over their severed heads on the way back.

He did not expect to survive this. But he would die content that he went down swinging his sword. As long as Marian led the people north, where the path was clear—

Robin was helpless to stop his sword arm dropping as he numbly half-turned in the direction of the Major Oak, where Marian's group had slowed down. People crashed into each other as they skidded to a stop.

As the thumping of horses' hooves drifted out of the trees and sailed into the clearing, Robin heard a voice he detested more than almost any other.

The Sheriff of Nottingham: 'Capture Marian! Kill the rest!'

Chapter Sixteen

The panicked murmuring of the civilians exploded into a riot of wailing and shouting at the blast of the Sheriff's bugle. Still looking north, Robin saw dozens of sergeants galloping on horseback through the forest, right into the Outlaws' camp.

The civilians broke apart and ran in every direction. Most of them did not reach the edge of the glade before being tackled to the ground by the Undead, who had lost their own jagged formation as the human banquet before them dispersed.

'No!' Robin cried, but there was nothing he could do. Everywhere he looked, another person was collapsing under the attack of an Undead. The air was shredded with the screams of the bitten, the chomping of rotting teeth through skin, the ripping of muscle from bone – the slick, wet sound of raw human flesh slipping down throats.

Fear stabbed at Robin. This was not an instinctive, mindless attack of the Undead, following the scent of living flesh all the way into the forest. It was a culling.

The Sheriff had come to hunt down any who knew

about the Plague. There must have been a hundred soldiers wearing heavy armour, with broadswords at their hips. They charged into the Outlaws, clubbing them with their shields and trampling any who fell beneath their horses.

'Little John,' Robin cried, 'with me!'

Side-by-side, Robin and the giant Outlaw pushed their way through the remaining civilians, who were moving in small circles, unable to run anywhere without scurrying straight into the arms of one of their enemies. Those who were caught desperately kicked and punched at their captors, but it was no use. Their grunts of effort became screams of agony within seconds.

Everything was a blur. Robin was just dimly aware of Friar Tuck swinging the blunt end of his staff at a sergeant as he galloped past; he barely noticed the Butcher joining him and Little John; he just about caught the sight of Much scampering up the nearest tree while a brace of fiends growled and grunted up at him.

Robin was aware of everything, and yet focused on nothing. His eyes were on the Sheriff, at the rear of his invading group, head turning this way and that as he surveyed the carnage.

Sergeants dragged women to show the Sheriff. The Sheriff leaned down in his saddle to look closer at each hapless victim; each time, he shook his head and the women were thrown back towards the Undead, who fell upon her like ravenous wolves.

He's looking for Marian, Robin realised.

'Clear a path to the Sheriff,' he called.

'Aye, Robin, sir,' said the Butcher, as he drove his spear into the thigh of a sergeant, stabbing so deep that he could not reclaim his weapon without dragging the armoured man right out of the saddle. His horse reared up and Robin leaped to take hold of the bridle, dragging his body into the saddle and turning the horse towards his enemy.

'Sheriff!' Robin bellowed, fighting to keep the sergeant's horse under control.

At the Northern edge of the glade, the Sheriff of Nottingham turned his head towards Robin. It was too dark now for Robin to see his eyes, but he knew the expression well – hateful, cruel, but fearful of his enemy.

Well, it will be the last *time you and I look into each other's eyes*, Robin vowed as he spurred his stolen horse into a gallop, left hand gripping the reins and right hand holding Will's sword. Civilians and

Outlaws clamoured to get out of Robin's way as he charged across the clearing.

With a roar, the Sheriff of Nottingham pointed at him. 'A thousand pieces of silver for the man who brings me Robin Hood's head!'

Sergeants converged on Robin Hood, swords raised and ready to hack, but Robin was too skilled a rider. With a jerk of the reins, he dragged his horse left, slashing at the nearest sergeant as he passed. Robin felt a moment of grim satisfaction as he heard the sergeant crash to the ground. He urged a burst of speed from his horse and galloped away. The charging sergeants crashed into each other as Robin raced away to the tree line on the Western edge of the glade.

Robin kept his eyes on the Sheriff, ready to strike him down. At six horse lengths away, and with his heart racing, he raised his sword..

But the Sheriff did not move, and did not even raise his weapon.

Why isn't he moving? thought Robin.

There was a flash as a figure with blonde hair and an icy white face flickered into view right in the path of Robin's horse, which reared up with an ear-rattling scream. Robin dropped his sword and grappled with the reins, desperately trying to control the beast, the forest blurring in confusion as his horse whirled around.

He knew who had appeared in front of him. Mother Maudlin had arrived in Sherwood!

Robin struggled in vain to control his horse, which bucked and threw him from the saddle. Robin tried to raise his arms but he was too late – he hit his face against a birch tree. The world dimmed. Pain lanced through his head as he span around in mid-air. He hit the ground face first and rolled down a steep bank into a muddy ditch.

By the time he stopped rolling, everything had turned a hideous black.

The Sheriff smiled to himself. Mother Maudlin may have given him cold shivers on occasion, but he could not deny that she had her uses. How easily the Witch had spooked Robin's horse, and removed him from the battle!

Now all he needed was to find the Lady Marian and he would make good on his debt to Prince John. The Undead would overrun the camp, and Robin would surely die. And when the Prince was king, he could look forward to the power and wealth of being the Sheriff of London.

He urged his horse on and trotted around the outskirts of the clearing, watching dispassionately as the Outlaws and the former citizens of Nottingham fought their losing battle against the rabid Undead.

Mother Maudlin walked beside him. 'Ah,' she crowed. 'There she is!' She pointed at Marian, whose sword hacked one Undead, then whirled to stab another. Even in broad daylight, the Sheriff thought, he would barely have been able to see her blade as it moved.

'She will defy you to the last!' Maudlin gleefully cackled. 'She will do anything to ruin your promise to Prince John, and your head will roll.'

The Sheriff let out a sigh which turned to mist in the chilly air. So much for Maudlin being helpful – now she was her usual taunting self. But the Sheriff was ready this time, because now he had a plan.

He looked the Witch in the eye. 'You might not be able to control people,' he said, 'but I'm rather good at it. Call off your fiends, stop the attack. Then watch this.'

He called out to the people following Marian out of he glade: 'We only want the Outlaw woman. Give her up to me and you will all be free to go. You have my word on this.'

Marian's followers shared anxious glances. For a moment, it looked like they would refuse until a burly serf broke from the group and wrapped Marian in a bear hug, pinning her arms to her sides. The Sheriff grinned.

'What are you doing?' Marian cried, as two more peasants joined the serf and wrestled her to the ground. A sergeant strode over with a length of rope and bound Marian's wrists and ankles. He picked her up, slung her over his shoulder and draped her in front of the Sheriff.

'We have what we came for,' cried the Sheriff to his men. 'Back to the city!' As the sergeants marched from the glade, laughing and joking, the Sheriff caught Mother Maudlin gazing at him – her face full of anger.

'These vagabonds have killed many of my babies. They must pay,' whined the Witch. 'You're not going to let them go, are you?'

'Of course not,' said the Sheriff, turning his horse and following his sergeants out of the glade. 'Turn your creatures loose on them. Swell your ranks in readiness for the Prince.'

Chapter Seventeen

Robin dreamed it was his first day as an Outlaw.

He dreamed he was back in the glade as a young man. He was looking up at the famous Outlaw, Will Scarlet, listening to every word, and memorising every lesson.

Will was young and strong. His hair was dark brown and his face merely weathered.

Robin dreamed of the lessons he was taught: how to swing a sword efficiently, and how to spar with perfect balance.

Of course, it made no difference how well Robin mastered his balance in those days. Will Scarlet was a fierce warrior and a smart fighter, and always upended his young protégé.

And each time Robin landed in a heap on the ground, Will would stand over him and say the same two words.

Get up!

Robin Hood stopped dreaming. His eyes snapped open, taking in his surroundings. He lay face down in the dirt at the bottom of a ditch. Above him dense trees whispered in the breeze. His head throbbed with a dull pain. He clutched his ribs, which hurt with each breath.

Get up!

He was powerless to obey Will's voice, which chased him from dreams to reality.

People are dying, *Robin!*

Robin turned his head, gasping with agony. Blood trickled down his temple and dripped on to the earth. As the fog of pain started to clear desperate thoughts filled his mind.

The Sheriff and Mother Maudlin were working together, and they seemed to have influence over the fiends. But to what end? And they had come for Marian!

He pushed himself up, his arms threatening to collapse under him. He pulled himself up to the top of the ditch and dragged his gaze towards the glade, dreading what he would see.

He saw no living people left in the glade, only dead ones. Robin tried to count the bodies. Torn limbs had been scattered all over the glade. Some of them were just bones now – the Undead had chewed right through clothing and flesh.

All Robin knew – the only thing he needed to know

– was that most of the people he was protecting were now almost certainly dead.

The Undead gathered in clusters as they gnawed at fallen bodies. He saw entrails spray as torsos were ripped open, the bloody debris falling on to the fiends like gruesome confetti. Here and there, demons butted heads over a carcass, snarling and snapping at each other like greedy dogs.

Only Mother Maudlin remained, strolling through the glade, her unearthly complexion shining in the moonlight. Her voice hissed a language that Robin had never heard before, but to which the Undead seemed to respond.

Then, on the other side of the glade, he spotted a familiar figure, scampering through the Undead, dodging their attacks and swinging a sword.

'Much,' Robin gasped.

Much was trying to get to Mother Maudlin, but his way was barred by Undead. He ran one way, and stabbed a fiend dressed as a yeoman through the neck. He ran the other and chopped off the head of a small boy whose gnarled hands were dripping with blood.

'I'll kill you!' Much yelled at the Witch, as an Undead lady in a half-torn kirtle lunged for him.

Robin's legs wobbled as he got up. He braced

himself against a tree, but he could not stop himself from collapsing. He looked up but could not see the young Outlaw. Had Much been overwhelmed?

He felt pressure at his left shoulder – a clawed hand about to tear into his flesh? He wheeled around, fists raised.

'It's me!' hissed the Butcher. He pulled Robin away from the glade, to where Little John stood, leaning against a birch tree. Their weapons and their Lincoln Green were awash with blood.

As they moved further into the trees, the Butcher handed Robin his bow, which had slipped off his shoulder when he was thrown from his horse. His quiver was still on his back, though Robin thought most of his arrows would be broken.

'Where's Marian?' Robin asked, his words painful in his throat.

'I don't know,' said John, helping the Butcher with Robin.

Robin's body was limp, and his heels made tracks in the earth as John dragged him away from the glade. 'And Tuck?' he asked.

'I don't know,' said John, using his axe to slash a way through the undergrowth.

'Much is still there! I saw him just a moment ago!'

cried Robin. 'We have to go back.'

'We can't, sir,' said the Butcher, who walked backwards with his spear held ready, and watchful for Undead.

'We must!' said Robin, trying to wriggle free. Little John took a huge handful of Robin's tunic, and shook him once. 'Everyone is dead!' he yelled. 'The fiends killed them all. There is nothing we can do.'

'It can't be true,' said Robin, shaking his head.

'But it is,' said John. 'Now we must leave. With luck, we might find Much and the Friar again.'

'And Marian? Did you see her escape?' Robin asked.

Little John and the Butcher shared a look, but neither seemed able to hold the other's eye. Robin felt his chest ache. He already knew the answer.

'The Sheriff took her,' said the Butcher.

So she's alive! Robin thought. 'Then we have to get her back,' he said.

'We can't, Robin,' said Little John.

'I'm not leaving her—'

The sound of crunching branches and flesh-hungry growls got louder.

'Here they come,' said the Butcher. 'Time to go!'

Little John looked Robin in the eye. 'All we can try

156

to do now is survive – as you said yourself.'

Robin nodded. If Little John could find it in him to keep going, then so could he. They set off after the Butcher, leaving their camp – their home for many years – behind them.

'Release me, you Norman oaf!'

Marian had made that demand so many times that the Sheriff had stopped bothering to tell her to be quiet.

She was draped across the saddle in front of him, tied at the wrists and ankles. 'Fine, don't release me,' said Marian. 'But untie me, and let us fight for my freedom.'

The Sheriff ignored her.

'I'm challenging you, Sheriff,' she said. 'You must accept. Or are you a coward?'

The Sheriff flushed with anger, but he kept his voice even. 'I am no coward, my lady,' he said. 'But I'm under strict orders not to ruin that pretty little face of yours.' He glanced down at the Marian, seeing her eyes widen. He smiled. *Now she knows why I snatched her from the battle.*

'No,' she gasped. 'Not... Not...'

'Yes, my lady,' said the Sheriff. 'You are still

betrothed to Prince John. He has decided to claim you.'

Marian tried to push herself free, but the Sheriff placed his hand on the back of her neck, keeping her pinned.

'What are you trying to do?' he asked. 'Break free so you can out-hop us? You would not make it five feet.'

Marian sighed, her body growing limp. 'I won't let it happen,' she said. 'I'll kill the Prince before I ever become his wife.'

'There's no use defying him now,' said the Sheriff. 'He will be King soon, and you will be Queen.' The Sheriff knew she would be a handful, but once he handed her over to the Prince, she would be his problem.

All the Sheriff cared about was keeping himself alive.

'To George's Bridge,' Robin called out as the three Outlaws ran deeper into the forest. Robin was frustrated and angry. His injuries slowed him down so much that he could barely keep up with Little John, let alone the Butcher – who was several horse-lengths ahead of them.

The trees crowded around them as they got closer to the River Idle, the canopy above their heads so dense the moon couldn't find a way through. Robin trusted his knowledge of the forest to guide him, and the sounds of the Butcher's steps ahead to tell him that his friend was still with them.

But an Undead fiend could be behind the very next tree he passed, and he would not know it. Not until the damned creature attacked him.

Keep moving. Stay alert.

He drew comfort from Will's voice in his head, urging him on, though his comfort was pierced with regret when he realised that he had lost his mentor's sword in the battle.

'Somehow, I'll make them pay, Will,' Robin muttered as he reached for a branch to swing himself left, towards the River Idle. 'I'll make them all pay.'

Robin almost lost his footing as the forest ground plunged into a steep slope leading to the riverbank. Beside him, Little John tripped and half-slid down to the water's edge.

The River Idle roared and rushed, the moon's reflection creating an oasis of light in the dark forest. Robin could clearly see George's Bridge, where two days before he and Friar Tuck had been fishing. He could see that the Butcher was already halfway across the wide oak log that formed the crossing over the water.

And he could see the pack of Undead charging out from the trees on the other side. The Butcher turned, almost tumbling off the bridge, and started running back towards him. But he was too slow. An Undead fiend grabbed his cloak with a gnarled hand and pulled him back.

Robin found speed that he should not have had, considering the pain he was in. *I won't lose another friend today*, he vowed. Little John wasn't far behind as they pounded down the riverbank, sprinting on to the bridge.

The Butcher kicked and punched as the Undead dragged him on to the opposite bank. He got to his feet and whirled around, skewering two fiends through their stomachs with his spear. He scrambled back on to the bridge as more Undead lunged at him from the side. Robin could see that his spear was too cumbersome for the quick, multiple strikes he needed to save himself; he knew his friend was doomed, but that was not going to stop him from trying to help.

An Undead child – a girl with plaited, blonde hair – rushed on to the bridge and sprang at the Butcher, planting the soles of its feet into his chest and digging its long nails into his cheeks. Robin drew to a stop three feet away, aghast that he was too late. Little John bumped into him and the oak trunk wobbled dangerously beneath their feet.

With a howl of agony, the Butcher used both hands to shove the fiend back. But the Undead girl's grip was strong, its feet dug into the Butcher's chest as they moved and swayed, locked together in a macabre dance.

The Butcher grabbed her forearms and yanked with all his might. The Undead girl's arms snapped at the wrists, but its clawed hands still clung to the Butcher's face. With a yell of defiance, the Butcher swung the fiend at the other Undead like a mace, over and over again, knocking fiends off their feet and into the river, where they sank beneath the frothing water.

The Butcher grew tired. He swung the Undead girl wildly, spinning his own body round and sending the child's carcass flying out of his grip and into the water.

'Butcher—'

The Butcher did not respond. As Robin reached out for him, his friend's eyes closed and he fell from the bridge, hitting the water and sinking out of sight.

The other fiends, numbering close to twenty by

Robin's reckoning, inched on to the bridge, their eyes turning hungrily on to Robin and John.

'Erm, Robin, sir...'

Little John was tugging at Robin's sleeve, drawing his horrified eyes away from the fiends who were starting to advance across the bridge. Robin looked behind to the other riverbank.

Back to where even more fiends were gathering.

Chapter Eighteen

How many are there, sir?'

Little John had a tremble to his voice. Little John was usually scared of nothing, but if anything was to be going to be the exception, this was it.

'I count twenty on my side,' Robin answered. 'And more than that on yours.'

'Well,' said Little John, 'however many there are, you don't have enough arrows.'

'I don't have enough for even half of them,' said Robin, as he and his friend edged their way to the centre of the bridge, standing back to back.

They watched as fiends closed in on either side.

'Then forgive me for saying, sir, but we are surely doomed,' said Little John.

From somewhere within Robin came a bitter laugh. 'It looks that way.' He felt a pure, cold rage inside him. He reached into his quiver – knowing from the weight that he had eleven arrows left – and barely lined up his shot before he let it fly.

Robin's aim was as true as ever. The arrow punched into the nearest fiend's head; the soft flesh and useless brains barely slowed it down as it continued its flight through the other side and disappeared into the darkness. The Undead man pitched forwards, hit the bridge face-first and bounced into the river with a splash.

Ten arrows left.

Robin half-turned to look at his companion, who stood with his double-headed axe held as ready. 'Our last stand, Little John,' he said. 'Fitting that it should be on the same bridge where we first met.'

Robin felt Little John's posture straighten against his back. 'Where I beat you in that friendly duel.'

'Ha!' said Robin. 'I *let* you win because I wanted you to join the Outlaws.'

'Keep telling yourself that, sir,' laughed John as he swung his axe. Robin heard the splash of a severed head hitting the river, then the body following.

Robin readied another arrow. Nine left. He looked back to the ragged line of the Plague Undead funneling on to the log bridge. In life, they would have seemed a most curious band – some wore tatty tunics, others ornate robes – but in Undeath, there was no such thing as hierarchy. Servants and masters were united in frenzy, as identical as kin with their empty eyes and pallid, boil-covered faces. Blood and drool dribbled over their slack bottom lips, while rotten flesh and muscle seeped out of jagged cracks in their skin.

The nearest fiend to Robin – dressed in monk's robes – had lurched to within eight feet of him. Robin swallowed bile when he caught a glimpse of its foot, seeing muscle and tendons spilling out of a small crater of decay – like a rancid stew bubbling over the edges of a pot. The Undead swayed this way and that, coming perilously close to falling over into the river without Robin even having to shoot.

The Undead were closing in on the Outlaws like moving walls of death.

Panic filled his chest like liquid fire, but Robin still did not lose the will to fight. He loosed his arrow at the Undead monk and almost cheered when he saw the top half of its head come clean off. The Undead man toppled like a lame horse, splashing into the river. Clumps of brain and flakes of skull rained softly on its lifeless body.

Arrow after arrow Robin loosed at the advancing Undead while, behind him, Little John's axe chopped heads from shoulders. Each shot of Robin's was true, ripping scalps off, revealing brains with the texture of sodden bread, and writhing with maggots and worms.

Soon the river was polluted with flakes of skin,

clumps of flesh, small puddles of dark blood and chunks of brain. The air was thick with the stench of death, wafting off the remaining fiends.

'I've no more arrows!' Robin called to Little John, as he tossed his bow and quiver into the river.

Robin felt the bridge wobble beneath his feet as Little John shifted his weight. He half-turned in time to see his big friend snapping his axe haft over his knee. He handed a length to Robin, who took it and readied himself for the next attack.

Another fiend came at Robin. It was dressed in a long gown, and black hair veiled most of its face. Its left hand was contorted into the typical Undead's claw, while its right missed a thumb and two fingers.

Robin half-stepped forward and swung his axe. The fiend's head flew off to his right, and its body toppled off the bridge to his left. But to strike at the Undead with the axe, Robin had had to let it move to within four feet of him, which meant that the very next fiend was already close before Robin could ready himself for another swing.

His blade caught the next Undead in the cheek, slicing through its papery skin between its top and bottom teeth. With a stomach-churning rattle, the fiend's jaw fell off and smashed into pieces on the wooden bridge, while the top half of its face fell back until it dragged its body down into the path of the next flesh-hungry creature, whose wheeling arms instinctively knocked it aside and sent it crashing into the River Idle.

But the fiends were so close now that Robin could not take a full swing. His elbows bent with every attack as the range shrank. His arm muscles burned with effort. He didn't have many more fiends to kill, but he was beginning to fear that his aim would fail him before he and John cleared a path to freedom. He was going to be overrun.

Beneath the hacking of his axe and the growls of the Undead, Robin caught the faint sound of a human cry. *Someone else is being attacked*, he thought. But the cry was not cut short. It continued, rising in pitch, volume and intensity.

It was not deep in the forest. It was getting closer.

And it was not agonised, but *angry*.

Robin bent his knees to keep his balance. The bridge was wobbling as the fiends advanced. Then the fiends in front of him fell off the trunk as something behind attacked them. The curtain of corpses cleared, revealing the Outlaws' saviour.

'Much!' Robin cried.

Chapter Nineteen

Much the Miller's son barely looked like himself anymore. Gone was the wide-eyed look of fear; in its place was a tight, steely glare, as he gestured with his sword to his Outlaw friends: 'This way!' he said. 'Come on!'

Robin Hood and Little John ran across the bridge to the other side, leaving five or six fiends scrabbling after them. But the Outlaws were too fast and their knowledge of the forest too good; with the nimble Much in the lead, using his blade to hack away errant branches and overgrowth, they covered a mile in ten minutes, by which time the Undead's snarling grunts and chaotic steps had long faded, swallowed by the forest.

Robin drew the group to a stop by a cluster of birch trees, the tangled branches and trunks locked in some kind of stalemate wrestling match. He embraced Much. 'I thought you were dead!' he said.

'Not me, but everyone else is,' Much replied, drawing away from him. His voice was quiet, his tone flat. 'The fiends feasted on everyone we saved from Nottingham.'

'I know,' said Robin, his head dropping. 'I should have listened to the Friar. Did you see what became of him?'

Much shook his head.

Little John punched the nearest tree. Robin felt a few leaves rain on him.

'What are we going to do, Robin?' asked Much.

Robin almost laughed. The boy still looked to him for guidance even after he had failed so spectacularly. Hardened he may have become, but tonight's massacre had not increased Much's common sense.

'Aye,' Little John chimed in, massaging his knuckles. 'What are you thinking, sir?'

Robin wanted to shout out that he didn't know, that he didn't trust his own judgment anymore. The silence dragged on. Robin fished in his brain for a thought, any thought, but his mind was as barren as a desert.

As if sensing his leader's hesitation, Much extended his sword out to Robin, hilt-first.

Robin gazed at it for a moment. It was a long sword, with a hilt studded with two rubies that glinted in the faint moonlight that crept through the canopy. 'Will's blade,' Robin breathed.

'I found it in the forest,' said Much, as Robin

numbly took it from him. 'I tried to kill the Witch with it. I failed.'

Robin nodded, his eyes on the blade. The scabbard was still wrapped around his waist, and he slowly, reverently slid the sword into it. It felt to him like it was weighted not only with steel, but with Will Scarlet's soul, and his disappointment in his successor. Robin could sense in the weapon the heaviness of his own failure, and felt it was only right that he carry the burden of the mistake.

Think it through, Robin.

Will's voice again, echoing in his mind, nudging him to a decision. 'We need to find a place which will protect us,' Robin said. 'Friar Tuck, God bless him, was right. We should have left. If he survived, he would have gone to Fountains' Abbey. That's where we will go, and let's hope others made it out with him.'

'We will be vulnerable on the road,' said Little John.

'Indeed,' said Robin. 'We'll stay in the forest as far as we can to keep hidden.'

'Then let's go,' said Much, not waiting for Robin to take the lead. He trampled on through the forest in the direction of Lincoln, and the two other Outlaws followed.

Robin tried to keep his mind clear as he walked. But no matter how great a distance he put between himself and the glade where his Outlaw followers and civilian supporters had died, the sounds of their screams and cries echoed in his mind as loudly as ever. And he suspected they would do so until the day he died.

However soon that day was.

Chapter Twenty

It took the surviving Outlaws three days to reach Fountains' Abbey on foot and, by the time they did, each one of them was ready to collapse from exhaustion.

As Robin, Little John and Much passed through the stone archway into the Abbey grounds, the afternoon sun hung low in the sky, casting long shadows. A monk in brown robes led a young ward out through the Abbey door.

'They don't look Undead,' said Little John, as Robin led them up the winding stone path that snaked towards the Abbey entrance.

'Doesn't even look like they've heard about what happened in Nottingham,' said Much. 'I expected the Abbey to be barricaded.'

Robin nodded. Life seemed to be going on very much as normal in Lincoln – which meant that no one from the doomed glade could have made it here.

Friar Tuck, then, was surely dead.

'Robin Hood!' cried a monk, hurrying over to the path and holding out a hand, which Robin shook.

'Brother,' he said, by way of greeting.

The monk pumped Robin's hand vigorously. 'Tuck said you'd come.'

All the tiredness drained from Robin. He released the monk's grip and took him by the shoulder. 'You've seen Friar Tuck?' he asked.

'Why, yes,' said the monk. 'He arrived last night. Looked like he'd had a tiring journey.'

'Take us to him,' said Much, his voice still flat and toneless.

'I'm not sure he's fit for visitors,' said the monk, with a frown. 'He, um...'

Robin felt the fear return. Was the Friar showing signs of the Plague? No, that couldn't have been it – he'd have changed by now.

'Is he sick?' asked Little John.

'No, no,' said the monk. 'He is fine, in body – except for his portliness, of course.' The monk chuckled, but bit it back when he saw that the Outlaws did not laugh. He looked at the ground. 'It's his mind. He talks of the world coming to an end, everything falling into darkness. It is really quite distressing. Abbot Henry has already talked of expelling him from the Abbey because he frightens the wards.'

'Take me to him,' Robin told the monk.

The monk knew not to offer any argument. 'Yes, yes... Come with me.'

The Outlaws followed the monk up the steps leading to the heavy oak doors of the Abbey. They walked through to the rear of the building and down the steps to the monks' dormitory. It was a one-storey extension to the main Abbey – a long, windowless room lined with two rows of ten beds facing each other. All the beds were empty except the one on which Friar Tuck was seated, cross-legged, his bald crown shining from the light of a beeswax candle on a shelf nailed to the wall beside him. In his lap was an open Bible, and on his ashen face was an expression of pure grief.

'He's tired from his journey,' mumbled the monk.

'Thank you, Brother,' said Robin, his voice low.

The monk bowed. 'I'll, um...give you some privacy,' he said and left the room.

As quietly as he could, Robin walked up the aisle and stopped at the foot of Friar Tuck's bed. 'My friend.'

Friar Tuck did not look up. 'You survived...'

'I'm not alone,' Robin told him. 'Little John and Much also escaped – both of them saved my life in doing so.'

Friar Tuck said nothing, he just turned the page of his Bible, but too quickly to have read anything. Robin's breath caught in his throat at seeing Friar Tuck so desperately reading through his scripture, without direction or purpose.

'It's not your fault,' said the Friar. 'There is no surviving this Day of Reckoning.'

'But we're still here, Friar,' said Robin gently. 'We're still fighting.'

'We're the Lord's loose ends, Robin,' Friar Tuck replied, turning another page, but still not reading. He looked up at Robin with eyes red raw from crying, though there was no emotion on his face other than resignation. 'His hand will pluck us from this lowly realm soon enough.'

Friar Tuck's head sank back down to his Bible. Robin gazed at him for a long moment, knowing that he could have shouted at the top of his voice and his words would simply pass through Friar Tuck's skull. There was no getting through to him now.

Robin turned and stepped out of the pool of candlelight, joining John and Much in the doorway and leading them back up the stairs.

He sighed heavily as he looked out across the fields spilling away from the rear of the great building, seeing a brace of monks in dirty robes, lugging sacks of vegetables towards the kitchen. They waved at him and Robin waved back, though he could not return their smiles.

'They work all day, them monks,' said Little John. 'They're great grafters.'

'What do we do now?' asked Much, as they sat on the grass.

'I don't know,' said Robin.

'What if the plague is spreading?' said Much.

'This isn't just a plague,' said Robin. 'This is something else. The Sheriff and Mother Maudlin... they're up to something. The Witch might be evil enough to wreak her black magic on people, but the Sheriff would not try to infect everyone in Nottingham without having something to gain.'

'But what?' asked Much, his tone flat and dead.

Not much will frighten Much, Robin thought, though he did not smile at his joke.

'I just don't know,' said Robin.

'There is something else we should be worrying about,' said Little John. 'The Sheriff and the Witch marched those Undead into our camp. Which means they can lead them somewhere else. This plague could spread much further than Nottingham.'

Robin stood up. 'People need to be warned,' he said. 'They need to be prepared.' He walked towards the Abbey.

'Where are you going?' called Little John.

Robin did not break stride. 'To see Abbot Henry.'

'Outlaw!'

Abbot Henry was a pale man at the best of times, but his face still drained of colour when Robin Hood appeared in the doorway of the chapter-house, the place where the Abbot and his monks conducted their administration, and discussed Abbey business. The air was thick with the smell of parchment, ink and burnt candle-wax.

Robin raised both hands, palm up. 'I shall stay in the doorway, Abbot,' he said. 'I assure you, I am not here to rob you.'

'Then why *are* you here?' asked the Abbot, stooping to fiddle with some paperwork on his desk.

'I mean no harm,' said Robin, staying by the doorway. 'I only wish to talk to you about our mutual friend.'

'If you mean Tuck,' said the Abbot, arranging the deeds into a neat pile, 'there is not much to say. The poor fellow's mind seems to have broken.'

'That's just it,' said Robin. 'It hasn't.'

The Abbot looked at him sharply, his frail hands setting down on the desk as he leaned forward, his cragged face sneering. 'What are you talking about, Outlaw?'

'Friar Tuck witnessed a series of very grave events,' Robin said. 'Events that would strain the heart and mind of even the most resilient man. He survived a Plague.'

The Abbot's eyes narrowed. 'What Plague? I have heard of no Plague.'

'It's true, believe me,' said Robin. 'I, too, saw it with my own eyes.'

The Abbot stood up from the desk, waving his hand dismissively. 'So you survived a Plague,' he said. 'Good for you. That alone does not explain why the Friar has become a blithering idiot.'

'He is convinced that this Plague is a sign of the Day of Judgement,' said Robin.

The Abbot shook his head as he sat back down. 'Tuck always was a bit melodramatic.'

'Nevertheless,' said Robin, as the Abbot absently drummed his fingers on the desk, 'Tuck has good reason to despair.'

The Abbot stopped drumming, his palm flattening on the wood. 'I think,' he said, 'that you better explain to me what you mean. Do step inside, Robin. But please, we do not permit weapons in the chapter-house.'

Robin unclipped his belt, standing Will Scarlet's sword against the wall outside. Then he took one step through the doorway. 'In Nottingham, there—'

'Have a seat, man.' The Abbot was pointing to the stool on the other side of his desk.

Robin sat down opposite the Abbot, whose crossed arms were hidden up the sleeves of his black robe. The crucifix necklace on his chest caught the final rays of sunlight creeping in through the window.

'What happened in Nottingham?' the Abbot asked.

'It was a Plague,' said Robin. 'But it was like no Plague any of us had ever seen or heard of before. It struck down its victims within hours, and then...' Robin paused, wondering how he would explain what had happened in his town.

What had happened to Will Scarlet.

'The victims do not die,' he said. 'Not exactly. They...endure, but in the form of the most vile, awful *things* you can imagine. They become flesh-hungry Undead who stop at nothing to devour any living person in their path.'

The Abbot looked at him for a long moment. 'Now

it sounds like *your* mind has broken.'

'Believe me, Abbot,' said Robin, 'I know it sounds mad, but I saw it with open eyes and a sober mind. In Nottingham, the dead are walking.'

The Abbot sighed, his cheeks puffing as he looked past Robin at the opposite wall, deep in thought. 'It's not quite what is prophesised for Judgement Day.'

'But you can see why Friar Tuck might have got it into his head—'

'Yes, yes,' said the Abbot, looking back at him. Robin felt relief fill him – the old man's eyes wore a quizzical expression. He was starting to believe what Robin was saying. 'But why has word not reached us? Why have we not been warned of the danger?'

'Because of the Sheriff,' said Robin.

The Abbot leaned forward. 'Explain.'

And so Robin told him the story, leaving out no details. By the time he was finished, the Abbot's face was paler even than before. Robin could imagine the thoughts that must be flying through his mind like a volley of arrows. Finally, he stood up and paced the chapter-house.

'So what do you want of me, Outlaw?' said the Abbot. 'You must have had a reason to have followed the Friar here.'

180

Robin half-turned his head. The Abbot was out of his eye-line; all he could see was the elongated shadow slung by the window in the wall behind them both.

'I seek guidance,' said Robin, 'and assistance. I wish for people outside of Nottingham to be made aware of the dangers. But I would rather not create a panic. We need people ordered, organised and in control of themselves. That is how we will survive.'

'But it's the Lord's will,' said the Abbot. 'Some will live...and some will die.'

If it wasn't for his view of the shadow, Robin Hood would have died right there and then, in the chapter-house of Fountains' Abbey.

The Abbot's crossed arms, nestled in the wide sleeves of his robe, shifted and sprang apart. Robin's reactions were instinctive, his right hand snapping out to grab the Abbot's left wrist. The blade was an inch from his throat.

Chapter Twenty-one

Still holding the Abbot's wrist, Robin let himself fall all the way back off his stool, dragging the Abbot to the floor and flipping him on to his back. He hit the ground hard, and Robin heard ribs cracking before he got to his feet and trod on the old man's wrist, forcing his hand open. He bent to scoop up the dagger and knelt across the Abbot's chest. He placed the point just beneath his eye.

'Why do you want to kill me?' said Robin.

But the Abbot didn't answer. Instead, he screamed out: 'Help! Help! The Outlaw is trying to—'

Robin didn't let him finish. He punched the Abbot in the temple, knocking him out cold. Robin shouted for Much and Little John, who came running to the chapter-house. They listened in horror to Robin's tale of what had happened, whilst they waited for the Abbot to regain consciousness. It took a few minutes.

'Wha...? Where...?' The Abbot massaged his head where Robin had punched him.

'You're still in the chapter-house, Henry,' said Robin.

The Abbot's eyes cleared as he looked to the doorway, noticing John for the first time; and at the young boy sat cross-legged on his desk, rifling through his papers.

The Abbot winced and rubbed his head some more.

Robin held out the dagger that had almost ended his life. 'I thought you didn't allow weapons in the chapter-house?'

The Abbot said nothing, he just glared furiously at Robin.

'So,' said Robin. 'I assume from your clumsy attempt to cut my throat that you're in league with the Sheriff and Mother Maudlin?'

The Abbot's eyes dropped.

Little John's voice was a breathy growl. 'You wretched, corrupt—'

'Oh, I think that our blessed Abbot here will seek forgiveness for his doings by telling us what he knows, so that we might put an end to it all,' said Robin.

'I'll tell you filthy Saxons nothing!' the Abbot spat.

'Oh, that does it.' Little John stooped down, reaching for the Abbot's robe.

Robin placed his hand on John's shoulder. 'Easy. I need him to be able to talk.'

The Abbot's face was split by a sneering smile. 'Yes,

you do,' he said. 'And I know that I'm too valuable for you to kill. So, go ahead – ask your pointless questions. You will get no answers from me.'

'You see this man here?' said Robin, tilting his head to Little John. 'Look at the size of him. He could lift you over his head and throw you from one side of this room to the other.'

'Very easily,' said Little John, slamming his right fist into his left palm.

The Abbot's smile did not fade. 'But you won't.'

'He could choke you until you were so close to death, Saint Peter would be waving at you just before we let you breathe again,' Robin continued.

Still the Abbot smiled. He even laughed. 'But you won't.'

Robin glanced at Little John. The Abbot was challenging them, and it was a challenge they would not answer – *could not* answer. Being an Outlaw was one thing – but to kill an Abbot in his own Abbey…?

It was never an option. And Abbot Henry knew it.

'Leave him with me.'

The voice startled Little John. Standing behind him was Friar Tuck. His face was clear of grief and confusion, his eyes determined and focused, his jowly face set tight.

Abbot Henry stood up. 'Tuck, I think it is time you took your ruffian friends away, don't you?'

'Oh, I'll take them away,' said Tuck, stepping towards Henry. 'Later.'

The Abbot looked from Tuck to Robin and back again. 'You, of all people, wouldn't try anything.'

'Wouldn't I?' said Tuck, backing Henry against the wall. Robin could see both of the holy men's faces. Both were pale, but for different reasons – the Abbot's face was white with fear, Tuck's with fury.

'I'm an *Abbot*,' said Henry.

'Yes,' said Tuck. 'That is your title. But you're a disgrace to that title – and a disgrace to the Church. I'm ashamed I ever called you my teacher. You aided the deaths of hundreds of people in Nottingham. I thought it was God's will, but it was not. God's will is for us to stop you. I wasted three days to despair – I am not wasting any more!'

Robin could have punched the air in triumph. His old friend was back, and more courageous than ever.

The Abbot was shaking his head. 'Tuck, think about—'

'I'll deal with Henry,' said the Friar, never taking his eyes off the Abbot. 'The rest of you, wait outside.'

*

185

'I would never have thought this of Tuck,' said Much, with a nervous laugh.

Robin, Much and Little John stood in the grounds, listening to the agonised cries of Abbot Henry sailing out of the window of the chapter-house. Here and there, monks heard the noise and walked as close as they dared.

'He's been in there a while,' said Much. 'That Abbot must be pretty tough.'

'Or very scared of the Sheriff,' said Robin.

'What do you think Tuck's doing to him?' asked the young Outlaw.

Robin shook his head. 'I don't know. But whatever it is, let's hope it makes Henry talk.'

Finally, the cries ceased. As the silence dragged on, Robin's heart soared – the longer Friar Tuck stayed in the chapter-house, the more the Abbot must be talking. And the more the Abbot talked, the more answers they would have.

But Robin had to give the old man credit – he was a tough fellow to withstand what sounded like a determined interrogation from Friar Tuck.

But Abbot Henry wasn't an especially tough fellow. That was what niggled at Robin as he heard movement from within the chapter-house and saw

Friar Tuck heading towards them. And as his friend emerged, Robin Hood might not have figured out the answer – but he had figured out the most important question.

'It's not just the Sheriff, is it?' he asked Friar Tuck.

The Friar shook his head, his eyes wide with fear. 'No, Robin,' he said. 'It's the King's brother... The Sheriff and Mother Maudlin are helping him to seize the crown.'

Chapter Twenty-two

'This is worse than we thought,' said Robin. 'A great deal worse.'

Tuck nodded. 'Henry was promised land and wealth in exchange for his support and silence,' he explained. 'The Prince has extended the same demand to other Abbots all over England. Barons and Earls too.'

'Indeed,' said Robin, running his hands through his hair. His mind was beginning to ache as much his body. Four days of chaos, battle, loss and travel with barely any sleep was beginning to tell on him. 'He would have contacted any and every land owner to bolster his claim to the throne. And he'll use the Plague Undead to scare those landowners into obedience.'

'So what does that mean?' asked Much. 'Do we have to assume that every Abbot, Baron and Earl in England is on the Prince's side?'

'We can assume,' said Robin, 'that any who said no to the Prince is now dead. Or Undead.'

Little John tutted. 'He knows King Richard would smash him to pieces if he tried to raise an army.'

'But John's fiends might just be a match for the

King's army,' said Robin, feeling the anger rise from his chest to his throat – a sickly, sour taste that he had to grit his teeth against.

'What else did the Abbot say?' asked Little John.

'That Prince John has received word of Richard's return,' said Tuck.

'And he and his army will have no idea what they're riding into,' said Robin. 'They'll be tired from fighting in the Holy Land, weary from travel…'

'They'll be slaughtered at the gates of London,' said Much.

'We must warn His Majesty. We will go into Lincoln to find some horses, and then ride south to head off the King – hopefully before he gets to London.'

Chapter Twenty-three

Five days later

From Fountains' Abbey, the Outlaws made for Lincoln on horses borrowed from the monastary. Five days later they were within a day's ride of England's southeast coast.

'Are you sure about this, Robin?' asked Little John, as the four Outlaws crested a hill in Hastings and continued their journey across a flat field. A grey sky hung overhead, and rain drizzled lightly on the weary travellers. 'What if we're riding the wrong way?'

'There are five ports in the southeast,' said Robin, on his horse that he had called Will. 'Dover, Sandwich, Hythe, New Romney... But our King will travel to London via Hastings.'

'Why?' asked Much.

'Because he's a proud Norman,' said Friar Tuck. 'He feels a connection to the site of his ancestors' conquest.'

'He sounds more like our enemy than our friend,' Much mumbled.

'King Richard may be a Norman,' said Robin, 'but he is as honourable and courageous as anyone I've ever known.'

Little John snorted. 'Unlike most of his kind.'

'Have you met the King, Robin?' asked Much.

'Long ago,' Robin responded. 'He was a Prince then, and he and his mother were guests of my father at Locksley. I was still a boy, and he was just a young man – but it was obvious he was a true warrior, even then. I knew nothing of combat at that age, and Prince Richard taught me how to hold a sword.' Robin laughed. 'I dropped it. Almost took off my own toes.'

'Will he remember you?' asked Much.

Robin sighed, looking across the fields of Hastings. 'We shall see.'

It was towards the end of the fifth day that the Outlaws stopped at the peak of a gentle slope and Robin's eyes fell upon a wonderful sight, half a mile away.

The camp of King Richard's Crusading army.

'This way!' he told the others as he steered Will down the other side of the slope and across the field. The camp was larger than some towns Robin had visited, made up of hundreds of canvas tents that housed the travelling warriors, who would no doubt be weary at the end of a long day's march.

As he got closer, Robin felt his own tiredness fall away from him. At last, fortune had favoured the Nottingham Outlaws – for the grass around the tents was marked by black scars where fires had burned. Many fires. King Richard's army had clearly been in Hastings for several days, which meant he had been resting his men.

They will go into battle strong, Robin thought.

And the troop of six knights who strode out from between the tents in a perfect formation certainly looked very strong. The muscles in their arms bulged through their chain-mail, and Robin could see the rigid contours of their plate armour beneath their dirty white hauberks. On the left sides of their chest were matching red crucifixes – the sign of them having 'taken up the Cross'. They wore sabatons on their feet that left marks in the earth.

'Halt!' Robin called to his fellow Outlaws, pulling hard on the reins to bring his horse to a stop a safe distance from the camp.

The knights marched towards them, hands placed casually, but confidently, on the hilts of their sheathed swords. They drew to a stop five yards in front of the horses. The tallest knight took a step forwards. His

complexion was dark, tanned by the hot sun in the
Holy Land. This close, Robin could see his face was
lined with deep scars, old and new; he was a man who
had seen war, and survived.

'What business have you here?' he asked.

Robin bowed. 'Good day, brave knight,' he said.
'I seek an audience with His Majesty.'

The Knight's face was impassive. 'Out of the
question.'

Robin could sense the tension among his followers
– anxious and mistrustful – and made a point of
keeping his own voice even. 'I beseech you, sir,' he
said, 'please inform the King that I bring grave news
from Nottingham.'

'News of a threat to the King?' asked the knight.

'Regretfully, yes,' Robin replied.

The knight gazed at him for a long moment, finally
pursing his lips and nodding as if concluding that the
raggedy traveller in front of him was neither a spy nor
an assassin. But, still protocol had to be followed.

'Will you be willing,' said the knight, 'to surrender
your weapons?'

Out of the corner of his right eye, Robin saw Little
John stiffen in the saddle, but he held the knight's gaze
as he nodded. 'Gladly, sir.' Robin unclipped the belt at

his waist and extended his sword. He saw Little John hold out his pair of axes, while Friar Tuck proffered his jagged staff. Much reached into his boots for his twin short daggers, extending them hilt-first.

Three knights stepped forward to take their weapons from them. The lead knight nodded when his companions had reformed their line. 'Follow me.'

The Outlaws left their horses at the edge of the camp and were guided through the rows of tents by the lead knight, who introduced himself as Sir Anthony. As they passed by, the resting knights – mostly highborn Norman warriors – eyed them curiously. Robin felt his usual hostility toward Normans rise up in his chest, and he hoped they could not see it on his face. These were Normans he was going to need on his side.

The King's tent stood in the centre of the camp. It was twice as tall as any of the other tents, and could have easily swallowed six of his Knight's makeshift dwellings.

When they arrived, Sir Anthony turned to face the Outlaws. 'I shall inform the King that he has visitors. Whom shall I say wishes to speak with him?'

Robin held the knight's gaze as he gave his birth name. 'Robert of Locksley.'

The Outlaws stood outside the entrance while Sir Anthony announced himself, before going inside. Robin could hear a murmured conversation, then the eruption of the King's booming, gravelled voice: 'Locksley? Get in here, man!'

Robin stepped into the King's tent.

It was a cavernous space, but the King seemed to fill it as easily and completely as the biting draught and prevailing damp. It was barely furnished, save for the King's bed and his weapons, which were arranged in a neat pile by the canvas wall. Richard the Lionheart stood to his full six-foot-five height – impressive and dominant in a way that even the physically grander Little John was not. He wore no armour, save chain mail, and yet matched Sir Anthony's bulk. The knight stood on the King's right, his expression a curious glower as he tried to fathom how the great King could know this Saxon peasant.

Robin ignored the knight, and fell to one knee. 'My King,' he said, head bowed.

'Sir Anthony tells me you bring grave news,' said King Richard.

'I do, sire.'

'Is it true,' said the King, 'that you are known by another name these days?'

Robin started to look up, then thought better of it. 'Yes, sire.'

'And what is that name?' asked the King.

'Robin Hood.'

On the edge of his vision, Robin saw Sir Anthony's Locksley. What danger could possibly await me there?'

Robin's gaze dropped. How was he going to tell the King what evil deeds Prince John had committed this bleak autumn?

But the King was perceptive. 'My brother,' he said.

'Yes, Your Majesty,' said Robin.

The King sighed and rubbed his forehead in irritation. 'I see,' he said. 'So, let me guess: he's been currying favour with some foolish Barons? Mustered an army he thinks can take on my noble Crusaders. Ha! My brother has always been half an imbecile. Tell me, Robin – what exactly has Prince John been up while I was away?'

So Robin told him.

'Do you expect us to believe that ludicrous story?' Sir Anthony's armour grated noisily as he shook his head.

It had taken Robin almost a quarter of an hour

to explain what had happened since the fall of Nottingham. He left out no detail, except how they had extracted information from the Abbot Henry.

'It is the truth,' Robin said. 'Prince John lurks in London, waiting for your return. His fiends will descend upon your army and tear it apart.'

'Nonsense!' Sir Anthony scoffed. 'You make it sound like we will ride right into Judgement Day itself.'

hand reach for his sword. Before he even gripped the hilt, the King's own hand had shot out to brace his wrist.

'At ease, Sir Anthony,' said the King.

'But, my liege—' Sir Anthony said incredulously.

The King's was quiet, and demanded total obedience. 'Do as I say.'

Robin saw Sir Anthony's sword arm drop, though he did not look at all at ease.

'So young Robert of Locksley became an Outlaw, eh?' said the King. 'I imagine your swordsmanship must have improved in that time.' The King laughed, and Robin could have almost jumped to his feet in relief.

'A longbow is my preferred weapon, Your Majesty,' he told the King.

'So I've heard,' said Richard. 'On your feet, Locksley.'

Robin rose to his full height. The King took a step towards him, Sir Anthony followed like a shadow. The Lionheart's face was unreadable, his eyes never leaving Robin's, but seeming to take in all of him so completely that Robin was surprised the King couldn't simply pull his dreadful warning out of his head.

'What is it you wish to tell me?' said the King.

'I must warn you,' said Robin, 'that danger awaits you in London.'

'In London?' Richard echoed. 'But it's my capital city,

'Is this true, Locksley?' King Richard asked.

'You cannot trust this man, my liege!' Anthony said.

'His eyes tell me I can,' the King said, his voice level, but brooking no argument. The King looked at Robin. 'But you must concede, Locksley, that Sir Anthony speaks sense. Your tale is an outrageous one.'

'I can only ask for your ear, sire,' Robin told him. 'What you do with the information is entirely your decision.'

The Lionheart nodded. 'But I do not believe that

a wily, cunning Outlaw would ride across half the country just to impart a warning. I'd bet on that Outlaw having a plan.'

'My plan was to trust your leadership,' said Robin.

The King of England looked from Robin to Sir Anthony and back again. 'My heart wants to believe you, Locksley,' he said. 'But my head says that there's no way my foolish brother could ever pull off a scheme the like of which you have described. And my head also warns me that I would be wise to be cautious. After all, you are an Outlaw. How am I to know that you're not here on my brother's behalf, seeking to fool me?'

'You don't, Your Majesty,' said Robin. 'I can only hope that you find it in you to trust me. I will understand if you do not.'

King Richard sighed again. 'Young Robert of Locksley is now an honourable warrior. I, of all people, know one when I see one.' He turned to Sir Anthony. 'Alert the men. We make for London. Locksley rides with us.'

Sir Anthony's face was tight with annoyance, but he bowed and said: 'As you wish, Your Majesty.'

At a curt nod from the knight, Robin bowed low to the King and made his way out of the tent. As he left,

Robin cast a look over his shoulder and saw the King sit down on his bed. His eyes seemed to stare through his tent, at something far away. Robin knew he was trying to imagine that what he had been told could even be possible.

Robin knew the King would have trouble doing that. Until he saw them with his own eyes.

'Listen to me, Outlaw,' said Sir Anthony, snapping Robin out of his thoughts. 'If this turns out to be a trap, I will make you pay. If *anything* happens to the King, I will make you pay. In this life, or the next. Do you understand me?'

Robin bit his tongue and counted to five, though he never looked away from the Knight. 'I understand,' he said.

Chapter Twenty-four

Two days later

'How do you know the King?'

Robin had given up hissing at Sir Anthony to be quiet. The knight would probably still find a way to talk even with his lips sewn shut.

They had entered London the second night after leaving the King's camp near Hastings. Inside the city, they kept to the shadows, moving as slowly and stealthily as they could, often crouching in dark corners for minutes at a time to be sure that any patrolling sergeants they passed would not double back.

They had seen no evidence of the Plague Undead, but even Sir Anthony admitted that there were far more sergeants on the streets of London than he had ever known. And when Robin assured him that he recognised many of them from Nottingham, but now wearing the sky blue and black colours of Prince John, the knight admitted that there might be something to Robin's story.

'But I don't see any walking corpses,' he said, for

what felt like the twentieth time.

They were creeping down Threadneedle Street, the brisk late autumn winds tossing around the smell of silk and cloth from within the closed-up shops, and almost veiling the sound of marching footsteps behind them until it was too late.

'Hide!' Robin hissed, grabbing a handful of Sir Anthony's cloak and dragging him into an alley. They flattened themselves against the damp timber.

'That's a lot of sergeants for a curfew patrol,' whispered Sir Anthony, his head cocked to listen.

'That's because it's not a simple patrol.'

Twelve sergeants stomped past the alley. They carried three unconscious people between them. Robin felt his stomach turn. 'They must have been snatched right from their homes,' he whispered. 'We have to do—'

Sir Anthony's voice was so quiet Robin could barely hear him. 'Oh no, no, no…' he said. 'That's twelve sergeants – *armed* sergeants.'

Robin clenched his fists in frustration. To sneak into London he and Sir Anthony had disguised themselves as peasants – which meant, they had no weapons but their wits. Not enough to tackle twelve of the Sheriff's men – and certainly not enough to tackle the Witch of Paplewick, who glided behind the sergeants. Her black robes blended with the night, and her pale face seemed to float, ghost-like, in the gloom.

And then she stopped, right between the two shops where Robin and Sir Anthony were hiding. Her smile faded to a pout of concentration.

Robin felt his heart take a dive. Did the Witch sense them, lurking there in the shadows? If she listened hard, would she hear them breathing? Hear their racing hearts? If she looked to her right, would she see through the shadows and pick them out?

Robin wished he had a weapon. If Mother Maudlin turned her head, they were done for.

The sound of the sergeants' footsteps on the road came to a stop, and a gruff Nottingham growl said: 'What is it, Mother?'

Mother Maudlin tilted her head back down and looked up the street at the sergeant. 'Nothing,' she said. 'Continue your march. We must deliver the meat to the Tower. My babies are hungry!'

Robin felt Sir Anthony tug at his cloak and he followed the knight as they stepped away from Threadneedle Street, keeping their backs to the wall.

Two questions sprung into Robin's mind. He knew that Mother Maudlin had sensed them, but she had not instructed her sergeants to arrest them. Why? That question, he could not answer. But he knew the answer to his second question with sickening, dreadful certainty.

Why was Mother Maudlin taking people to the Tower of London?

She had said it herself.

Her babies – the Undead – were hungry.

Chapter Twenty-five

A pale dawn had risen over London and the surrounding suburbs when a tired and sluggish Robin and Sir Anthony left via the same gate they had entered late the previous day. They walked, and occasionally jogged, the three miles east along the River Thames, where they met two of King Richard's knights who waited with their horses. Together, they rode to Essex, where the King's army had remained – close to London, but still a safe distance away.

There was no camp – no tents or telltale fires. Richard the Lionheart wanted no sign of his impending arrival if he was going to launch a surprise attack on his own capital city.

The King, fully armoured and straddling a magnificent white horse, broke from the snaking line of knights and soldiers. He rode out to meet Robin and Sir Anthony. Robin tried to spot his Outlaw brothers, but he could not see them amongst the mass of knights and infantry.

'What news?' the King asked.

Robin let Sir Anthony speak first, for the report of

a sceptical knight was likely to carry more weight.

'Strange goings-on in London, sire,' said Sir Anthony. 'The sergeants patrol at the command of a pale-faced woman. An ungodly looking creature with an unholy star etched into her forehead.'

Robin saw the King's eyes widen beneath his steel helmet. 'So it is true?' he said. 'My brother is in league with Mother Maudlin?'

'I do not know her name,' said Sir Anthony. 'But she certainly looked like a witch to me.' He half-shrugged and half-shuddered. 'I didn't think witches were real.'

King Richard looked past them both, his eyes distant. 'They are, my friend,' he said. 'Believe me. They are.'

'On the Witch's instructions,' Sir Anthony continued, 'the sergeants carried unconscious civilians to the Tower of London.'

'She's feeding them to the Undead,' said Robin. 'For now, the Undead are confined to the Tower.'

King Richard leaned forward in the saddle. 'Of course,' he said. 'My brother is not so stupid that he would just let the fiends overrun the city. He'd have no one to rule over – and that boy is desperate to rule over *someone*.' He paused a moment, then turned his horse around. 'Come,' he said. 'We have work to do.'

'My brother will stay in the Tower,' said the King. 'He knows it's the safest place for him when I return to London.'

Robin and Sir Anthony knelt either side of the King, who had a map of London laid out on the road, his helmet and sword placed over the corners to keep it pinned. Richard's hand moved over the map as he made his points.

'That is where he will be,' he said. 'And he will have him full force with him – living and otherwise.'

And John will have Marian with him too, Robin thought, with a shudder. *His 'Queen-in-waiting', held captive somewhere.*

'You see the problem?' the King asked Robin.

'I do,' Robin answered. 'Behind the Tower's walls, the Prince has the advantage.' He hesitated, wondering if he truly could give voice to his thoughts. Since his failures in Nottingham, his doubts about his own tactics had been like a heavy boulder on his back. Since deciding to stand up to the adversity they faced, to not simply roll over and wait for death, he had felt that weight lessen with each passing day.

But it was one thing to vow that he would go down fighting. It was something entirely different to ask the King of England to trust him when his crown, throne and *life* were at stake.

'We must try,' he said, trying to sound as confident as he could. 'Otherwise, many lives will be lost.'

'What do you think, Sir Anthony?' Richard asked.

The knight rubbed his scarred cheek. 'Our problem is maintaining the element of surprise,' he said. 'The Tower is within the city walls, and we cannot pass through one gate as an army – it will take too long. By the time we are upon the Tower, Mother Maudlin will have unleashed the Undead, and Prince John will have mustered his men. We could be crushed.'

The King's lips curled in a thin smile. 'This all sounds very dangerous,' he said. 'I'm starting to like it.'

Robin stole a look at the knight, whose eyes seemed to say: *If the King does not make it out of this battle, it will be your head on the block.*

'We must exploit the weakness of the Tower,' said Richard, tapping his finger on the map. 'See here.' He pointed to a crude marking on the Tower's moat, where a bridge crossed it at the west. 'It only has one entrance. We must storm it from there. If our archers shoot volleys over the walls, they might give us enough cover to charge a great number of men into the grounds. As long as we make it from the city gates to the Tower quickly, my brother might not have sufficient time to react.'

Sir Anthony shook his head. 'But we'll be trapped in the Tower grounds, with Heaven knows how many of those *things* the Outlaw describes.'

The King was rolling up the map. 'So we'll kill them.'

'But—'

'Sir Anthony, please,' said the King. 'You're making my head hurt. Now come, both of you – we have a city to reclaim.'

Chapter Twenty-six

'It will be a miracle if this works,' said Little John to Robin. The Outlaws rode at the head of Richard's group, with five knights alongside them, armed with longbows.

They were to be the first wave of King Richard's invaders. Much and Friar Tuck were fifty yards behind, among the soldiers, awaiting the King's command to charge.

Robin tore his gaze away from the Ale-gate, an entrance to London's east that was drifting into view ahead, a hazy arch in the morning mist. Robin knew that the mist would give them some cover as they made their approach, but not a great deal. They were putting their faith in luck as much as tactics.

'Even if it doesn't work,' said Robin, 'I'll die happy knowing I killed as many of the Undead as I could.'

One of the knights, a man of Robin's age, with a thick blonde beard and deep brown eyes, looked across at him. 'What are these Undead like?' he asked uneasily.

Robin didn't know how to answer, except to tell the

man: 'They're not invincible. Aim for the head and they will die just like the living do.'

The knight's gaze turned towards the city. He did not look any more confident than he did before.

Robin glanced over his shoulder at the King, at the head of his army. Richard nodded once, and Robin dug his heels into Will's flanks. 'Now!' he said to the others.

Robin, Little John and the five knights galloped forwards. The tall spires and towers of the London churches, scattered across the city, pierced the mist. They rushed towards the stone walls – a hundred yards away, he could see the sky-blue cloaks of five city sergeants at the gatehouse, and the two dozen on the walls.

And if Robin could see them, that meant they could see him.

In one motion, Robin dropped the reins and slipped his longbow from his shoulder. Will pounded forward as Robin took an arrow from his quiver. He loosed his arrow and smiled grimly as it pierced a sergeant's neck, sending him tumbling from the battlements into the moat. Robin gripped his charging horse with his thighs as he readied another arrow. The thunder of hooves and the war-cries of the knights made his heart pound with excitement. His companions drew back their bows and let fly their missiles towards the panicked sentries.

The sentries raised their crossbows, but the King's attack had taken them by surprise and they were slow and confused. Screams ripped the air as six of them fell to the invaders' arrows, their hands clutching at their wounds. So far, not a single crossbow bolt had come Robin's way.

The sergeants at the gatehouse stood rooted to the spot, staring aghast as the knights charged at them out of the mist. They drew their swords to fight – but then they seemed to think better of it, and fled into the city.

'John!' Robin called. 'Kill them. Don't let them close the gate!'

'Aye,' John called back, taking aim.

Robin loosed his arrow, watching it cut a straight course until it punched into a sergeant's back, flinging him to the ground. Two others fell, and another only made it ten yards before he too was cut down.

The last sergeant ran in a zigzag pattern, hoping to avoid the shot he knew was coming.

'Allow me,' said Little John. His shot was straight as ever, the arrow slicing into the sergeant's neck, skewering him. The sergeant half-turned as his legs collapsed beneath him. Robin could see that he was dead before he hit the ground.

The Ale-gate was now unguarded. This was their moment.

'Forward!'

The voice of King Richard was as loud as if he was a mere few yards behind. At another volley from Little John and the knights, the remaining sergeants on the walls ducked down behind the battlements.

'We can't let them warn the Prince,' said Robin as he nocked another arrow. He was just ten yards from the gate now. 'Cut them all down!'

Robin saw the first sergeant scramble out of the gatehouse and away down the narrow road into London, his cloak billowing behind him. Robin drew Will to a stop on the far side of the dank moat. He took aim.

Thwack-thud!

The sergeant fell with an arrow in the side of his face. He landed on top of two of his compatriots, their bodies like a small funeral pyre.

'We surrender!'

The remaining sergeants tossed their crossbows to the ground and stepped into the archway, hands raised. Robin dismounted, nocking another arrow and training it on the sergeants, whose eyes were wide as they looked at the army charging towards London.

'The King has returned,' one of them gasped.

'That's right,' said Robin. 'And your master will be driven out of London. I suggest, you run out of your own accord.'

The sergeants looked at each other, unable to believe what they had been offered. 'You'll let us go?' said the biggest of the group, a burly man with a Nottingham accent. Robin felt his jaw clench and told himself: *You have more important matters at hand.*

'Yes,' he said. 'Leave your crossbows on the ground, and get as far away from London as you can. You're responsible for many deaths because of the orders that you followed, and you will pay a price one day. May death find you wherever you run.'

Heads bowed and hands still raised, the surviving sergeants slipped past Robin, John and the knights and scurried to one side, out of the path of Richard's army as it passed though the gate. The thundering of hundreds of horses' hooves sent tremors through the ground.

'Good work, Locksley,' called Richard, as he galloped past. 'Ride with me!'

Robin swung himself into Will's saddle and guided him into the stream of rushing knights, coming up alongside Much and Friar Tuck.

'Good shooting, Robin!' said Tuck.

'Now let's storm the Tower!' cried Much.

The streets of London were winding, criss-crossing like tangled tree branches. On the main streets, traders stood dumbfounded beside market stalls as the Crusaders rampaged past them. Robin heard shouts of: 'God save King Richard!'.

The army's progress down the narrow streets was slow. The smell of wattle and daub houses, with their old straw rooftops, was heavy in the damp air as the army cut its course through the city, unchallenged by sergeants.

The King's forces turned on to Tower Hill, approaching the gate of the Tower of London from the North. A thousand of the King's returning Crusaders and the four Outlaws converged on the great, stone fortress like a human avalanche, their horses' hooves churning up dust as they battered the ground.

They raced alongside the deep moat that had been dug in front of the earthwork, topped by a wooden palisade – the vulnerable 'western wall' that the King had spoken of earlier. Unlike the stone walls, there was no elevated position for crossbow-wielding guards to watch from. There were narrow gaps between the wooden poles of the palisade, through which Robin could see dark flutters, like shadows. Armed guards were scurrying around behind the wooden fortification, criss-crossing the Tower grounds, arms waving desperately. Several of them were running to the gate, trying to drag it closed.

'Dismount, dismount,' cried the King, slipping from the saddle. 'We must charge on foot! The Bridge will not support our horses!'

The King, Sir Anthony and scores of knights drew their swords as they raced across the bridge, their battle cry deafening. The bridge – not much more than a wide row of thick logs tied together with blackened rope – bounced and wobbled beneath the weight of so many men.

'Archers!' Robin called, dismounting and readying his bow. 'Cover the King!'

Within seconds, the invaders had sent a storm of arrows arcing over the palisade. Across the bridge, the King and his lead knights slammed their bodies against the Tower gate, trying to force it open.

'Again!' Robin called, as another volley sailed over the walls. More and more knights with swords were hurrying across the bridge to bolster the King's forces, making a human battering ram that slowly forced the gate open.

'We have to get inside the walls,' said John, who was nocking another arrow beside Robin, 'before the Undead come crawling out of the Tower.'

Across the bridge, the clash of steel on steel as the King's men did battle with the guards inside the gate pierced the air.

'We will trust His Majesty,' said Robin, readying another shot. 'Our job is to give him cover.'

'Mine isn't,' said Much, who stood behind Robin and John. Behind him, Friar Tuck was still in the saddle. 'If Mother Maudlin's in there...' He pointed to the Tower.

'No, Much,' said Robin, loosing his arrow, which joined the small cloud of others that soared over the palisade. 'We must maintain discipline. You must stay close. I will not lose another Outlaw.'

'She betrayed my father,' said Much, drawing the sword gifted him by one of the knights at Hastings. 'I want my revenge!'

'Wait!' said Robin, but it was no use. Much charged across the bridge and disappeared among the King's men.

'We'll find him, Robin,' said Tuck, as he climbed down from his horse. 'We will all make it through this. Justice is on our side.'

Robin looked towards the Tower. He could see the four turrets of the citadel – three of them square, one of them circular. It was the most monstrous, intimidating fortress Robin had ever seen – a three-storey keep built by William the Conqueror, about a hundred-feet wide and ninety-feet tall. And inside it were God only knew how many of Mother Maudlin's Undead.

Marian may be in there, too, he told himself. He heard a cheer go up from the invading knights as they defeated the guards and flooded through the open gates.

'No more arrows!' Robin called to the archers. 'Swords! Make for the gate!'

Robin hooked his bow over his shoulder. With John and Tuck either side of him, he drew Will Scarlet's sword and ran over the bridge.

Chapter Twenty-seven

The Tower grounds were little more than a trampled grass ring around the keep. But there was not much grass to see beneath the two walls of fighters – Prince John's men in sky blue; King Richard's men in white overgarments with their blood-red crosses – colliding with each other in a chaos of clashing swords and shields.

At the King's command, his army spread out across the grounds, driving the Prince's men back. Robin fought his way to the front line, to King Richard's left. Sir Anthony was at his right. To Robin's left, were John and Tuck. There was no sign of Much.

Robin swung his sword as two sergeants lunged for him. He saw a flash of glinting steel in the corner of his eye, and veered away from a third sergeant, coming in from his blindside. He let the sword drift past him, catching the attacker's wrist and twisting it. The sergeant screamed as he dropped his sword, and Robin dragged the edge of his own across the man's throat, blood spraying upwards as he sank to the ground with a wet, desperate gurgle.

'Come on!' Little John was roaring, as he chopped and hacked at any who dared attack him. Friar Tuck was parrying and thrusting with loud grunts, his chubby face as red as the blood that Robin had just spilled.

As more of the King's knights stormed through the gate, Robin was pushed forward by the human current, finding himself shoulder-to-shoulder with the King, who was using his broad blade to drive his enemies back.

'Where are these fiends, Locksley?' he said. 'I would have expected them to be unleashed by now.'

'Me too, sire,' said Robin, slamming a punch into the nearest enemy face, feeling a nose crumble beneath his knuckles. 'But I promise you – they are here.'

'And they'll eat you alive!' said one of their enemies. Robin felt his heart lurch when he saw the thin-faced man, with a pointed nose that resembled a rat.

Prince John, in the flesh!

He was grappling with Sir Anthony, their blades pushing and grinding against each other. 'When Maudlin unleashes the Undead on you, you will regret you ever came back to London. This is your last day, Lionheart!'

The King roared and brought his blade round. His

swing was awkward because of the crush of people. The edge of his sword missed the Prince, and slashed down the face of a gap-toothed sergeant next to him. Robin saw his eyeball disappear among the flailing limbs. Screaming in agony, the sergeant fell to his knees and was trampled to death within moments.

'You'll pay for this, little brother!' Richard yelled. 'I swear to that!'

'England is mine!' Prince John shouted back.

'Keep fighting!' Richard called to his men. 'Destroy the Prince's pitiful army!'

Robin looked to his left. There were half a dozen people between himself and Friar Tuck, who Robin could see was being forced aside as more and more knights charged towards the front line. Tuck brought his blade up to parry an enemy strike, kicking out with a thick leg and hitting his attacker in the groin. The man doubled over, and one of his fellows lunged, stabbing his sword at Tuck's face. Tuck flicked his sword upwards, but his deflection was weak; a deep gash was slashed in his face above his jaw. Blood streamed down his face. He continued fighting, but he swung his sword slowly.

He's tiring, Robin thought, his heart a block of ice amid the heat of blood and battle. He looked past the

Friar at Little John, who tirelessly stabbed and sliced anyone in front of him. 'John!' Robin called, ducking back away from the front line, feeling Richard's knights move past him like an unstoppable sea. Robin was moving against the tide, his chest squeezed and crushed by the press of bodies.

Little John did not hear him.

'John!' he gasped. 'Make way!' His words were overwhelmed by the battle cries and snarls of exertion. Tuck's sword was still slashing from side-to-side.

At waist height.

'John!'

Little John did not hear him.

'Keep pressing!' the King shouted. Robin was lifted off his feet as the knights pushed forwards.

Robin's sword arm was pinned to his ribs. 'John! Help Tu—'

A flash of steel lit up Robin's vision for a moment. The Friar's whole body froze, then juddered in pain. His limbs went slack and he dropped his sword. As his killer drew his weapon back, he slumped to the ground, disappearing among the bodies.

Friar Tuck was dead.

The sword that killed him was held by a familiar face.

Chapter Twenty-eight

'Sheriff!' Robin called.

The former Sheriff of Nottingham, dressed in the sky blue of Prince John, could not hear him over the roar of battle. Robin could see from the gleam in his eye that the Sheriff was cheering his own small victory against one of the Nottingham Outlaws. Finally, he had taken one down.

Robin barged his way forwards. He stormed to the front line and swung his sword at the Sheriff, who blocked with his kite-shaped shield.

'Robin Hood!' he yelled, his voice strangled by the wall of noise all around them both. 'At last, I can kill you!'

'I dare you to try,' said Robin, stabbing low, dragging the Sheriff's shield down, and then flicking his blade up, nicking his neck. The Sheriff tried to back away, his teeth clamped together as he breathed heavily, angry and frightened all at once. The Sheriff lunged, his blade stabbing for Robin's face. Robin stooped beneath it and swung his sword two-handed at the Sheriff's thigh.

The Sheriff wailed in agony as his leg was severed from his body. He collapsed as blood gushed from the stump so fiercely that his compatriots were distracted long enough to be run through by the blades of the knights.

Robin stayed in a crouch as he moved forward. The Sheriff was on his back, his chest heaving in rapid, wheezing gasps. Already, the colour had drained from his face.

He was dying quickly.

'That was for Tuck,' said Robin. He placed the edge of his blade against the Sheriff's throat. 'And this is for the citizens of Nottingham.'

'You'll never get her out of the Tower,' said the Sheriff.

Robin froze. 'What?' he said. 'Marian? Tell me where she is!'

The Sheriff laughed, blood and spit flying from his lips. 'Oh, I'll tell you,' he said. 'She's in the northwest turret, kept prisoner by the Prince. She's in the Tower, with the Undead. There's no way out for her. You may win this battle, you may even defeat the Prince. But I can die with a smile knowing that your heart will be broken.'

Robin pulled his sword away from the Sheriff's

neck and stood up, turning away from him as the blood and breath and life leaked out of his body for good.

The Sheriff died as he wished to – with a smile.

His heart pounding, Robin's eyes roved over the battlefield. The King's men were charging forward all around him now, the mass of people breaking apart as the Prince's depleted forces fled. The knights hunted them down, killing them one by one. The cry of 'Victory!' rang out around the Tower grounds.

Behind him, Little John was crouched beside Tuck, cradling his head. Tears streamed down his face as he looked at Robin, stunned and ashen. 'What happened?' he asked.

Robin looked him right in the eye, unblinking. 'His death is avenged.'

Little John laid Tuck's head down on the ground, and placed his hands over his chest. Then he stood up. 'And Much?'

Robin shook his head. 'I don't know.' He turned back to the Tower, the great white fortress. His eyes found the northwest turret, where the Sheriff had said Marian was being kept.

'We have to get inside,' said Robin.

'Inside the Tower?' said John, eyes narrowed. 'Are

you mad? The Undead are in there.'

'We'll take the Tower soon enough.'

Robin and Little John turned to see King Richard coming towards them, dragging the limp body of his brother by one ankle. He dropped the Prince and stood before Robin.

Robin pointed at Prince John. 'Is he…?'

'Dead?' said the King. 'No, he's not dead. I'll decide what to do with him later.' He shouted for two of his knights, who hurried over. 'Take him out of here. Keep him in custody – do not let him wake up and run away.'

'Yes, my liege,' said the knights.

'He should pay the price,' said Little John.

'He will, my good man,' said the King. 'But I will decide the price.'

'We must take the Tower, sire,' said Robin. 'Marian is in—'

The three men covered their ears as an unnatural shriek ripped through the air around them. All over the grounds, the remaining fighters froze in mid-strike. Every pair of eyes looked to the Tower, to the northwest turret. Mother Maudlin, her black robes fluttering in the light breeze, her white-blonde hair blending with the pale sky behind her, stood on top of the Tower. She spread her arms and tilted her head back, sending up her hissing, snake-like call.

The doors to the Tower yawned open and the Plague Undead burst out with snarls and growls.

Chapter Twenty-nine

They were not just spilling from the door. More of the Plague Undead rushed around the southwest turret, coming in all shapes and sizes, and all ages and classes.

'Yes!' shrieked Mother Maudlin. 'Yes, my babies! Kill them all!'

'To me!' the King shouted. 'Reform the lines.'

The King's knights hurried towards him to form ranks, as the fiends rushed, their arms wheeling and their faces set in hungry snarls. Robin saw the King go pale. Beside him, Sir Anthony – whose face had picked up a few new scars – looked similarly stunned.

'Demons,' he gasped.

The King readied his sword. 'I don't care what they are,' he said. 'This is my Tower, my city, *my country*. And I'm taking it back!'

Robin instinctively reached for his longbow, but all he grabbed was his own shoulder – he must have lost it in the battle.

'Remember, sire,' Robin told the King. 'Decapitate them or destroy the brain – it's the only way to kill them.'

'Chop off their heads!' called Richard, the command passing among his men.

Robin and Little John were on the front line with the knights – all of them weary, but ready to fight.

The Undead ran towards them. They had no tactics, no objective other than to kill. Kill and consume. They were falling upon King Richard's army like rain.

'For Tuck,' Robin whispered.

'And for Much,' said Little John.

We don't know he's dead, thought Robin.

With a roar that burned his throat, he brought his sword down as if it were an axe, cutting the first fiend in half from skull to waist. It fell apart like a curtain, revealing more and more of them rushing at the Crusaders.

King Richard sliced at the fiends as easily as if he were hacking at wheat. The severed corpse heads rained on the army.

'Don't let them scratch or bite you!' Robin called, as he swung his sword left and right, plunging into skulls and faces. He knew his arms must have been tired. He knew his muscles must have been aching.

But he felt none of it. He felt nothing but the will to survive.

A pair of clawed hands reached for his face. Robin

slashed his sword, the blade tearing easily through the rotting skin and bone of the fiend, leaving behind jagged stumps. King Richard reached across Robin to drive his own blade into the fiend's gaping mouth. Robin's sword crossed the King's as he pierced the skull of a lady fiend, her green kirtle stained with blood, brain and pus.

But there were so many of them.

'Back!' called the King. 'Back – keep the distance.'

Richard's army moved back. Strangled cries told Robin that some had been caught, some had been scratched. His heart sank, but he kept fighting as furiously as always. The Undead were crushing forwards, rotten arms swiping at the air and each other as they moved forward in their ragged, chaotic line.

But the King's army was fighting back. Heads flew. Soggy brains slapped chain mail and plate armour. Corpses collapsed in a heap of rotting flesh and bones.

'No!'

Mother Maudlin, still perched on the northwest turret, stabbed a finger at the air. 'You will pay for this, Outlaw! I promise you… You will *suffer*!'

The Witch disappeared in a flutter of black robes.

'Marian,' said Robin. He broke from the line and

began driving forward.

'Robin!' called Little John, as Robin whirled his sword one handed, left and right, like he was clearing the undergrowth of Sherwood Forest.

'What is he doing?' Sir Anthony's voice was incredulous and growing faint as Robin moved further and further away, closer and closer to the Tower.

Deeper and deeper into the sea of Undead.

The King's voice was furious. 'Locksley, you lunatic!'

Robin forced his way out the other side of the Undead horde, his momentum making him stumble. He lost his balance on the dead body of a sergeant and fell in a heap. By the time he had stood up, a brace of fiends had sensed him, and began scurrying towards him, running so fast that their rotten skin was flying off their limbs.

Robin turned and ran towards the turret. He charged through the door and slammed it shut behind him. He felt the fiends batter against it and heard them scraping their nails on the wood. He knew it wouldn't hold for long. He grabbed a torch from a sconce on the wall and held it so he could see.

To his left, a stone passageway led into the keep. To his right, a narrow spiral staircase climbed upwards.

Robin decided to try the stairs, taking them two at a time with his torch held out in front of him, the flames arcing back with the faint breeze, driving back the darkness, revealing the next steps, the blur of the curving stone walls...

...and the face of a fiend.

Robin reared back, almost losing his footing as he braced himself on the wall, nearly burning his face with the torch.

The fiend was dressed in a ragged cape of a Tower guard, though it wore no armour. Its claws dragged along the stone walls either side of the staircase. Its face was lined with the familiar boils, though most had burst. Pungent yellow pus drained out, the stench worsened by the heat of Robin's torch.

Robin regained his balance and took a couple of steps down, maintaining the distance between them. He jabbed his flaming torch at the fiend, thrusting the end underneath its flailing arm and catching the hem of its cape. It caught fire and the flames devoured the fabric. Up and up the flames licked, catching the fiend's pallid skin and climbing up into its dirty hair, which ignited and burnt to nothing in seconds.

Robin took another step down the staircase as he watched the flames curl around the fiend's head like a bonfire. Its skin turned black almost instantly, the charred, dead flesh sliding off its skull and hitting the stone steps with dull slaps.

The fiend's skeletal face was completely exposed, glowing an obscene white in the darkness. Robin felt a thrill of triumph as the fiend's cranium fell apart, tumbling to the steps revealing the mushy ball of grey that used to be its brain. But his thrill was punctured when he saw the fiend's teeth gnash together, its half-rotted tongue lashing around inside its mouth as it emitted the same hungry growl.

It was still not completely dead.

With a roar of revulsion, Robin swung the flaming torch at the fiend's head one last time, the flames catching its brain, which sizzled and smoked, before exploding in a shower of grey sludge that coated the walls. Robin threw up his sword arm just in time, feeling the slick scraps of organ slapping against his elbow.

Robin stepped aside as the fiend fell face first into the stairs. Robin heard what was left of its empty skull shatter on impact, the broken shards outpacing the dead *thing* as it rolled down the stone steps.

Robin shook the brains off his arm and continued up the steps, finally coming to a heavy wooden chamber door. A thick timber beam ran across it, supported by iron brackets.

Robin set down his sword and unbarred the door. Almost immediately, it was wrenched open from the inside. Marian stood there with her fist poised to strike. She froze. 'Robin?' she gasped.

'We have to go,' he told her, stepping into the chamber – an empty, circular cell with two slit-windows in the walls.

'You survived,' she said, her face lighting up.

'I did,' said Robin. 'The Prince has been captured, and the King's men are fighting the last of the fiends. It will be over soon.'

Marian ran past him to the chamber doorway, bending to pick up Robin's sword. 'Let's go,' she said, disappearing around a curve in the staircase.

Robin made to follow, only to bump into her as she came back up the stairs into the chamber. 'Back!' she said.

The echoing sound of fiends growling and grunting drifted up the staircase.

Chapter Thirty

Marian moved to close the chamber door.

'Don't!' said Robin. 'There's no way out of this chamber, except down those stairs. If we close the door, we're as good as dead.'

Marian's eyes widened in incredulity. 'As opposed to *now*?'

Robin held his flaming torch in both hands. 'They can't all get through the doorway at the same time,' he told her. 'If we fight hard, we might be able to kill them one by one. But if we shut ourselves in here they'll break down the door and flood the room.'

Marian nodded her understanding. They stood at the top of the stairs and waited for the fiends to attack.

The first fiend, a peasant woman with one arm missing, came scrabbling around the curve in the staircase. Robin jabbed it in the face with the torch, and before the flames had stopped ripping off the fiends' skin and flesh, Marian stepped forward to plunge the sword into the Undead woman's skull. Its brains exploded and splashed into the faces of two more fiends clambering up the stairs not three feet behind.

The Undead peasant toppled backwards, halting the progress of those behind, and giving Marian enough time to lunge forward and chop off both their heads with one vicious swing.

'Drive them down!' said Marian.

Robin walked in step with her, down the stairs as she hacked at the flailing clawed hands of the Undead. A flurry of fingers flew in all directions; blackened blood trickled on to the stone steps. The narrow staircase tossed around the echoed growls and grunts of the Undead until its awful sound was the only thing Robin was aware of.

Robin poked and prodded at the fiends with his torch, reaching over the first line of dead creatures to burn those behind them. He sets scalps on fire, the flame burrowing through soft skulls and singeing useless brains that burst in a shower of slop.

But still they came.

The clamouring Undead clawed and shrieked as they fought to get to their victims. Robin stepped in front of Marian, swinging his torch like a club, hitting the fiends in the face. Flames ripped off their lips, noses and scraps of their cheeks, which splattered on the opposite stone wall.

But still they came.

The sword in Marian's hand swished and slashed as she whirled it at the Undead, sending craniums spinning into the darkness below. Robin went to her side, thrusting desperate kicks at the nearest fiends, and feeling his foot plunge through a chest, the ribs crunching, and the flesh stretching and breaking as his foot emerged on the other side. He dragged it back, feeling sick and exhilarated at the same time.

They were doing it. They were driving the fiends back and they were fighting their way down the stairs.

After what felt like an eternity, the grunting and growling of the Undead attackers ceased. There was no sound in the stairway except Robin and Marian's exhausted, heavy breathing. Robin's chest burned as hot as the torch in his hands, which he could barely hold up, so tired were his arms.

Marian let the sword fall beside her with a clang as she sank into a sitting position, running both hands through her sweaty red curls and smoothing them away from her face.

Robin reached down to take her arm. 'We can rest when we're clear of this Tower,' he said. 'Come on.'

With a groan, Marian got to her feet, listlessly

picking up the sword again.

Instead of the stone staircase, there was now just a steep slope of piled bodies, most of which were coated in lashings of black blood and clumps of brain. Robin gave his hand to Marian as she stepped up on to the hideous mound, staying close to her as he followed. He had to duck his head to make sure that it didn't scrape along the ceiling, prodding each body with his foot to be sure that it would support his weight.

After ten careful paces, Marian was clear, hopping down to the steps to continue her descent, sword held cautiously in front of her as she disappeared around a bend in the stairway.

Robin tested the last Undead stepping stone with his left foot.

A gnarled hand stabbed up out of the pile and closed around his right foot. He cried out in surprise, falling awkwardly. Panic rose like bile in his throat.

One fiend was still not dead.

'Robin?' he heard Marian call as he tried to yank his foot clear, succeeding only in helping the fiend who clutched him break free of the heavy blanket of corpses that crushed it. Robin kicked and flailed, but the fiend would not let go.

'Robin!'

Marian leaped over his head on to the mound of bodies and brought her sword down over the fiend's forearm, severing it and breaking Robin free.

Robin crawled away, almost rolling and falling off the pile of bodies, fighting to right himself so that he did not risk snuffing out the torch. Marian hopped down off the bodies on to the stairs, passing Robin on the way down.

'Can't turn my back on you for two seconds, can I?' she said with a weak smile.

They reached the bottom of the stairs. 'We shouldn't risk it,' said Marian, listening at the door through which Robin had entered the tower. 'They're still fighting out there and we'll be cut off from the King's forces.'

Robin nodded. 'Let's find another way.'

He looked at corridor leading into the keep. He could only hope that they would find another way out somewhere in this fortress.

'In here,' he told Marian, as he barged open the first door that they came to. It was made of good timber, but it opened easily. Robin and Marian slammed the door shut without turning to see what type of room they had entered, barring it with a thick wooden beam.

The two Outlaws turned around and took in

their surroundings. A ring of twelve stone columns, connected by perfect archways, flanked rows of long wooden benches. A narrow aisle led to a pristine marble altar. On the altar was a golden crucifix that reflected the light of the beeswax candles placed either side of it.

'This must be St John's Chapel,' whispered Marian. 'My father told me about it.'

Robin looked around and saw a sight to give him a surge of new energy. Directly opposite, just behind the altar, was a wooden door. With any luck, it would lead outside to the Tower grounds, where they might be able to skirt the fighting and rejoin the King.

'Come on,' he whispered, leading Marian up the aisle.

'Oh, no... Don't rush off so quickly.'

Robin and Marian were startled by the unexpected voice. Mother Maudlin emerged from behind a stone pillar to the left of the altar. She stepped slowly, confidently into the middle of the aisle. Her pale blonde hair seemed to consume the reflected light of the candle, giving her ghostly visage an even eerier look as she walked towards them.

Robin held his sword out. 'Don't take another step, Witch!'

Mother Maudlin stopped dead in the middle of the aisle, fifteen feet away from them. 'Fine,' she said, and before her echo had stopped cannoning off the stone pillars, she was standing right in front of Robin, her hideous grin wider than ever. 'I won't.'

Robin and Marian stumbled away from her. Robin fumbled with his flaming torch, which slipped out of his grasp and rolled away out of reach.

The Witch laughed. 'You didn't say I couldn't move *at all*.'

Robin felt Marian tense behind him as they took up a defensive position beside one of the pillars, ready to duck behind it if they had to.

Thud!

The heavy wooden door rattled. Robin knew what the sound was without Mother Maudlin having to tell him.

'They are here,' she said, her face gleaming with the pride of a parent. 'You are the reason I lost most of my babies... You will pay for that now. Pity you two won't be enough to go around.'

Robin looked helplessly around him. He saw something move in the shadows behind one of the pillars. Robin's eyes flicked to Marian. She returned his look. She had seen what he had, behind the pillar to Mother Maudlin's left.

'There is one thing I don't understand,' he said, to keep her talking. 'You created a whole army of these creatures. Why did you use them only to help Prince John?'

The Witch's look was withering. 'I was helping myself,' she snapped. 'Do you honestly think the Prince could have controlled me?'

'You had no plan, did you?' said Robin. 'You created these things for no reason. You just wanted to cause death and destruction. You're pure evil.'

Mother Maudlin smiled. 'And what of it?'

Thud!

The battering of the Undead at the door continued.

'You will pay,' said Robin. 'For an eternity.' He felt his fist clench as he hoped that Marian was preparing to make the move he needed her to make.

'In your dreams, Outlaw,' said Mother Maudlin.

'Go back to Hell!' Marian screamed, swinging her sword. The blade did not connect with Mother Maudlin, only the air where her neck had been moments before.

'Nice try,' said the Witch, reappearing at the pillar just to her left. 'But I'm not *that* stupid.'

Robin grinned, victory in his heart. 'Oh, but you

are, Mother. You really are.'

Much the Miller's son sprang from behind the pillar, burying his two short daggers into her back. A gasp escaped the Witch's lips as she grew still.

'That was for my father,' said Much.

Robin took a step forward, scooping up his dropped torch and standing before her.

'As the lady said – go back to Hell.' He touched the flame to the hem of her long robes. The flames swarmed her body in seconds. Robin, Marian and Much took a step back as the Witch fell to the floor in a burning heap.

Robin clapped Much on the back. 'I was wondering where you'd got to,' he said.

Much smiled. 'I came searching for the Witch.'

'And you found her,' said Marian.

'We were fortunate that you ended up in here,' said Robin.

Much stared at the ground. 'Yes, well… I got lost.'

The three of them laughed, as much in relief as in humour. 'I think,' said Robin, 'we should start looking for a way—'

Thud! Thud! Thud!

The door to the chapel was beginning to splinter.

'Come on,' said Robin, running to the back of the

church and trying the second door.

It was locked.

'What now?' asked Much.

Thud! Thud! Thud!

'We fight,' said Robin. 'We haven't come this far just to die now.'

Thud!

They stood ready for the moment that the Plague Undead would burst through the door.

Chapter Thirty-one

But they did not come. Instead, silence fell. Robin led his companions forward, inching past the burning body of Mother Maudlin.

'Did they...give up?' asked Much.

Robin shook his head. 'The Plague Undead never give up.'

Thud! Thud! Thud!

The door was creaking, cracking, swelling. Any moment now, and it would give.

Thud! Thud! Thud!

'This is it,' Robin said to them. 'Be ready. Kill them all!'

Thud! Thud! Thud!

The door flew off its hinges into the benches and bounced off with echoing clatters.

Standing in the doorway were King Richard and Little John.

'Locksley!' boomed the King. He wore the broadest of grins.

'Much!' said John, barging past the King and striding into the chapel. He hugged the boy tight.

'I can't believe you're alive!'

'He killed the Witch,' said Robin.

'Is that right?' said Richard, walking into the chapel, followed by his knights, Sir Anthony among them. He nodded at Robin, a thin smile on his lips. 'Well, then, we'll have to see about rewarding you handsomely, lad.'

Much stepped aside from Little John, offering the King a low bow.

'Is it over?' Robin asked.

'The fiends are all dead,' said Richard. 'All of them.'

Robin felt Marian's hand squeeze his. 'England is safe again,' she said.

'Yes, it is,' said Richard. 'I'm glad I trusted you, Locksley. You have helped set England free, and driven off the most serious threat to my Kingship that, God willing, I will ever face. I am in your debt. Anything you want, and it is yours.'

Robin looked from Marian to Much, and then to Little John. He suddenly felt very tired.

'Honestly, sire?' he said. 'I just want to go home.'

Epilogue

With London – and England – now safe, Robin Hood and his Outlaws returned to Sherwood Forest, which they continued to protect as the fallen city of Nottingham began its rebirth. They would go down in legend as England's most courageous and revered Outlaw heroes.

Having reclaimed his capital city, King Richard decided to discipline his treacherous younger brother, but stopped short of having him executed – following the example of their father, King Henry, who had once forgiven the young Richard for rebelling against him.

Prince John would never again try to take over England using zombies.

Of course, history books might offer a different version of the events in England of 1194. And, yes, maybe it didn't happen *quite* the way it did in the book you have just read.

But is it not more fun this way?

BLACKBEARD'S PIRATES
VS
THE EVIL MUMMIES

*He was dead, his mouth open in a
scream of unimaginable terror...*

When Blackbeard steals cursed
treasure, he is taken from the high
seas to hostile Egyptian deserts...
How will Blackbeard and his
pirate crew survive in a deadly
battle against evil mummies?

Don't miss this next Mash Up –
coming in July 2011!

978 1 40831 389 3 £5.99 PB
978 1 408 31550 7 eBook

www.orchardbooks.co.uk

ORCHARD BOOKS

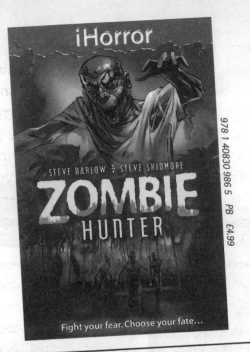

iHorror

STEVE BARLOW ‡ STEVE SKIDMORE

ZOMBIE
HUNTER

978 1 40830 986 5   PB   £4.99

Fight your fear. Choose your fate…

iHorror: Zombie Hunter
Sneak peek

You have been contacted by Mr Romero Price, head of the Nutco Oil Corporation. His company is based on the South Pacific islands of Saruba and Panuka. Saruba is well known to you. For hundreds of years tales from the island have told of the dead rising up out of their freshly dug graves in the form of zombies. But you've never actually been to Saruba. These living dead creatures are difficult to destroy and will not stop hunting for living flesh to feed on.

Mr Price claims that zombies are now highly active on Saruba, which is affecting Nutco's ability to harvest the nut crop grown on the island and processes it into oil. As you are the world's expert at dealing with zombies, he has promised to pay you a substantial sum of money to destroy the zombies on the island and to find out where they are coming from. Of course, you have accepted the challenge and are looking forward to once again fighting the creatures of the supernatural.

You have packed the weapons and equipment you think you will need to destroy the zombies, and have flown your private jet to the South Pacific.

There is nowhere to land your jet on Saruba, so you fly to the airport on the neighbouring island of Panuka. Your request for permission to land is granted. But the descent is a bumpy one. Dark storm clouds are gathering as you approach the runway – lightning flashes across the sky and you wonder if this is an omen of what is to come...

✦ *Go to 1 (it's on the next page)*

1

Heavy rain lashes down as you land your jet and taxi towards the arrivals building. You bring the jet to a halt, power down the engines and open the door. As you descend the steps with your bags, a tall man approaches you, holding out one hand, and carrying a large umbrella in the other. You are surprised to see that, despite the pouring rain, he is wearing sunglasses.

The man introduces himself as a representative of Nutco Oil. "Mr Price has sent me to collect you. He is very anxious to meet you," he says in a strangely slurred and hollow voice. "Nutco's HQ is in the hills of Panuka, so we'll be flying there by helicopter. Please come this way."

He helps to carry your bags to the waiting helicopter through the pouring rain. You stow all of your bags except your case of weapons. You slide this on to the rear seat next to you, put on the helicopter's communication headphones and settle down to enjoy the ride. The man takes his seat in the front and fires up the helicopter's engine.

Soon you are in the air and heading towards the HQ. The weather is getting worse – visibility is limited and lightning crackles across the sky, buffeting the helicopter.

"Do you think we should turn back?" you say to the

pilot through your communication mic.

The pilot shakes his head. "Relax – just take it easy. This is going to be the ride of your life – or rather, your death!" He turns round, takes off his glasses and gives you a skull-like grin. Your stomach lurches as you stare into two pus-filled, maggoty eyes – the pilot is a zombie! He laughs manically and thrusts downwards on the controls, sending the helicopter diving towards the ground.

‡   *If you wish to fight using your martial arts skills, go to 11.*

‡   *If you wish to use your flame gun, go to 75.*

‡   *If you wish to shoot the zombie, go to 29.*

TO BE CONTINUED IN

iHORROR:
ZOMBIE HUNTER...

ANTHONY
HOROWITZ
HORROR

Collection of horror stories by No 1 bestselling
author Anthony Horowitz.

It's a world where everything seems pretty normal.
But the weird, the sinister and the truly terrifying are
lurking just out of sight. Like an ordinary-looking
camera with evil powers, a bus ride home that turns
into your worst nightmare and a mysterious
computer game that nobody would play...
if they knew the rules!

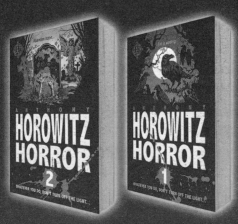

ORCHARD BOOKS
www.orchardbooks.co.uk

Don't miss Jiggy McCue's next
adventure in the 17th century!

MICHAEL LAWRENCE

JIGGY AND THE WITCHFINDER

Jiggy's got some amazing ancestors –
make sure you discover them all...

OUT NOW!

jiggymccue.com   wordybug.com